ALEC BIRRI

Inspector Vazquez: The Beginning

First published by Near Future Nighmares 2023

Copyright © 2023 by Alec Birri

This novel is entirely a work of fiction. The names, characters and incidents portrayed in it are the work of the author's imagination. Any resemblance to actual persons, living or dead, events or localities is entirely coincidental.

First edition

ISBN: 9798376244104

This book was professionally typeset on Reedsy. Find out more at reedsy.com

Contents

Chapter 1

Detective Sergeant Emiliano Vazquez studied the latest missing persons' list, and compared it to the previous copy. It was twice the length. How the police were expected to investigate them all, he didn't know.

Emil made a calculation. '1995.'

The desk officer looked up. 'What?'

'At this rate, in eighteen years time Argentina's entire population will have gone missing.' He turned the lists towards the corporal. 'So if it's 1977 now, we'll *all* be dead by 1995.' The officer shrugged and carried on reading his newspaper.

Emil put down the lists and deleted those names he had previously investigated – pointless going over those again as any backhanders from the families would have long since dried up, even if the bodies had yet to be found.

It was always a body. Never a case of mistaken identity, a runaway returned home or released kidnap victim. If you went missing in South America these days, that's how you stayed.

But then, chasing ghosts was all the police could do, and thanks to the military junta's determination to wipe out the communists, there was always a plentiful supply of those

1

desperate to find out why their fathers, sons and occasionally, daughters had stopped coming home. Families themselves sometimes disappeared, but the investigation of them was strictly off limits to a newly promoted sergeant in the *Policia Federel Argentina*. They invariably involved government-backed militias and messing with them was one surefire way of finding yourself on a list – of one.

Emil set about reducing the new names to the few he would 'investigate'. This was the tricky bit – trying to work out who was likely to pay the most without stepping on any toes further up within the police, never mind some mob with connections. It meant there was never any decent money to be had of course – the wealthy took their bribes straight to the top, but there was always the odd doctor or solicitor's family that could be good for a few pesos.

That took some investigating of its own, however and it started with a process of elimination. Emil struck his pen through each of the peasants – no money there. Likewise, he deleted those identities with known communist connections or other criminal records, before moving on to the laborious but potentially lucrative part; a methodical search of the Buenos Aires telephone directory.

That took care of the rest of his shift, and by four o'clock Emil had six names – all professionals: a dentist, solicitor, teacher and three businessmen. He could take a month's salary from that little lot in just a day if the families lived close enough. Leaving the notepad on his desk, Emil approached a wall map of the city.

'Good work, Sergeant.'

Emil's heart sank and he mouthed an obscenity before turning back to face his boss.

Inspector Gomez had the notepad in hand, and was studying the names. 'But I think it would be better if I dealt with these. The families of dentists and solicitors can be very judgmental of junior police officers and I might be able to get more out of them.' He looked at his Sergeant. 'If you know what I mean.'

Emil knew what he meant alright – the higher the rank, the more the families were prepared to shell out, but he would be lucky to receive the equivalent of a day's pay let alone a month once the inspector had taken his cut.

The desk officer grinned at Emil's misfortune and the inspector pounced on it. 'What are you smiling at? Get back to work!' The corporal struggled to stay on his seat. Gomez motioned for Emil to join him in his office and closed the door once they were inside.

'It's called 'RHIP', Sergeant – rank has its privileges. I'm sure you'll understand once you get to my position.' He offered Emil a cigarette but then withdrew the packet before he had a chance to take one. 'Or perhaps you reckon on having enough money to retire before then?' The packet was offered again.

Emil hesitated before taking the Marlboro. His boss lit it, and then his own.

The young sergeant recognised a veiled threat when he encountered one. It wasn't that Emil feared any physical harm or indeed disciplinary action – selecting what to investigate based on the potential of bribes was endemic within the police – no, what worried Emil most was being shut out of any future opportunities if his loyalty could be called into doubt. Ensuring his boss had received a fair share of gains in the past was academic. For the first time Emil's superior had seen what he was planning. If the inspector did carry out the 'investigations' himself and managed to get more than expected, then that could spell trouble for Emil. RHIP indeed.

Emil became contrite. 'No, Sir. I've always known where I stand with you and would like to think my sergeant would do the same for me when, er, I mean, *if* I get to become an inspector.'

Gomez ignored the answer and studied the names again. His lips moved in silence as if working something out. To Emil's surprise, the notepad was then offered back to him. But he couldn't take it.

'I need you to investigate something else first.' Gomez released his end of the pad and walked over to a map of the country. Emil groaned to himself as the inspector pointed to a location in the foothills of the Andes mountains – a good two days' drive away. Emil became positively nauseous when he found out what he had to do.

'There's an abortion clinic operating under the guise of an orphanage in the village of Ariloch.' Gomez turned to his junior. 'Go there, find out what's going on, arrest and charge those responsible, and shut it down.'

Emil was grateful for the return of the list, but not with what was basically a local matter. Given the distance, a week would be needed and he had bills to pay now – zero bribes in peasant country. Communist guerrillas hid out in those hills too and army or police, they didn't care who they killed.

Emil tried getting out of it. 'What's wrong with the local police? Why aren't they dealing with it?'

Gomez gave a look that indicated he didn't tolerate his orders being questioned but answered anyway. 'They were until one of the mothers decided to abort her children *after* they were born and I believe that's called murder so homicide has become involved.' He regarded Emil with suspicion. 'Unless of course you don't want to do any *real* police work?'

Of course Emil did and that included risking his life but not if the infanticides turned out to be at the hands of some inbred incapable of understanding her actions. Packing her off to a nuthouse was hardly a result to be proud of and certainly not one worth dying for. It might technically be murder, but there were way more serious crimes than the mercy killing of some half-dead incestuous runts. The people were little more than animals up there, anyway.

Emil's sigh was more visible this time. 'Is there a pathologist's report?'

The inspector burst out laughing. 'The country's at war, Emil. We're dealing with a dozen bodies a week thanks to the antics of the Reds. There aren't enough pathologists for that let alone the dead sprogs of a village idiot. Not that you need a medical degree to recognise a bullet through the head.'

It seemed to dawn on Gomez the risk he was asking his sergeant to take. 'Look, I tell you what. Give me back the list and I'll make a start on it. It will give you something to look forward to while you're away. You know I'll be able to make more er, *progress* than you.'

As if Emil had a choice in the matter. For all he knew the abortion clinic was a ruse to get him out of the way so Gomez could keep the backhanders to himself. Emil tore out the page and handed it over.

'Who's going with me?'

The inspector bit his bottom lip. 'We can't spare anyone at the moment so you'll be on your own.' Emil's eyes widened and was about to protest when his boss interrupted. 'Don't worry, I've arranged for a relay of police and military escorts to get you there and back in one bit.'

Emil felt a little better but thought the transport plan bizarre.

It was almost as if he had to get there no matter what. Emil was used to strange orders from his boss, especially now the government was having to clamp down so hard but that was usually because some rich family was paying through the nose for protection, but why the same fuss for a bunch of penniless peasants?

Gomez passed him a file. 'Here – you can read up on the case during your journey.' Emil counted the pages – both of them. Barely more than a map and a couple of contact details.

The inspector extinguished his cigarette and opened the door. He grabbed his sergeant's arm as he was about to leave. 'Some priest will want to give the kids a decent funeral once you're done.' Emil was pulled closer. 'Make sure he buries *everything*.'

Chapter 2

'Sergeant Vazquez?'

Emil stopped and glanced around. He'd already spotted the padre's cassock a couple of hundred metres further down the track, but being recognised out of uniform was worrying. The pastor closed the distance to Emil and smiled as he stretched out a hand.

'I'm Padre Martin. Welcome to my parish.'

Emil's eyes flitted left and right as if expecting an ambush, but empty scrubland between the two men and the foothills in the distance made that unlikely. He shook the pastor's hand, but Emil was still nervous. He wanted to put a hand on his pistol, but the padre kept a firm hold while expanding on the welcome.

'And on behalf of the people of Ariloch, I hope you enjoy your stay with us.'

He let go. Nothing bad happened, so Emil relaxed a little. 'How did you know it was me?'

The priest laughed. 'Ariloch is twenty miles from the nearest town with little to offer the weary traveller so we don't get many visitors and when we're told to expect one, we like to make him feel welcome. Can I help you with your bag?'

Emil pulled it further up onto his shoulder to indicate he didn't and looked past the padre. The village couldn't be seen so Emil guessed there was still some walking to do. The military truck had dropped him a mile back so it couldn't be that much further. 'Didn't we arrange to meet in the church?'

The pastor faced the direction of his parish, Emil spotting the cross on top. 'I thought it best to escort you on the final part of your journey. The *Dirty War* has made the villagers nervous and they sometimes don't take kindly to strangers.' He turned back to Emil. 'Especially if they're military or police, so it might be better if I introduce you as my friend, 'Mr' Vazquez.'

Emil nodded. Fair enough – anything to break down barriers. His official status would have to be revealed at some stage, though.

The remaining twenty minutes of the journey was spent discussing the extent of guerrilla activity in the area, or at least what the padre had seen or been made aware of. Emil was relieved to hear that although the police station in the nearest town had been attacked, no outsiders had been seen in Ariloch for years.

He still wanted to be in and out as soon as possible, though. 'Mr' Vazquez or not, it was only a matter of time before some enterprising villager decided a few pesos could be made as an informant and even the most pious of priests could be susceptible to that.

They were about to enter the village when Emil spotted someone attempting to hide behind a tree. Emil took out his handgun.

The padre put a hand on top of it. 'It's only Pedro.' He called out. 'It's okay, Pedro, come and meet my new friend.'

Emil holstered the weapon as a boy of about ten gingerly approached, unable to take his eyes off where the padre's new friend had hidden the pistol from view.

'Say, hello to Mr Vazquez, Pedro.'

One of Pedro's arms was deformed and Emil's natural suspicions became sidelined for pity. He bent down and put out a hand. The boy cowered so Emil leaned forward a little more. The weight of the Browning pushed down on the left side of his jacket, exposing the hand grip. Pedro grabbed it and ran.

'Fuck! Fuck!' Emil dropped his bag and tore off after him. 'Idiot!' Emil cried out loud as he quickly became outpaced. The boy was like a human monkey the way he bounded over brooks and fences. Pedro was soon out of sight.

'Fuck!' Emil said again when he stopped in the middle of what appeared to be the village square. Emil was out of breath and had to place his hands on his knees to recover. 'Stupid, stupid idiot!' Looking at the ground, Emil continued to admonish himself for the rookie mistake.

It was only late afternoon, but the sun was setting behind the Andes, and shadows edged into Emil's field of view. He looked up. A group of about twenty children stood before him.

The padre arrived and deposited Emil's bag at his feet. He wasn't as out of breath and just needed to mop his brow to recover. 'I'm sorry about that, but don't worry, we'll soon get it back.'

The padre addressed the children, but in a dialect so thick it was impossible for Emil to understand. Four of the youngsters shot off in different directions the moment he finished. Peering at Emil's bag, the padre said, 'I hope you have something to reward them with when they return your property.'

Emil thought there was next to no chance of getting his handgun back but then realised his second rookie mistake – not bringing any candy for bribes of his own. Emil thought of what he did have. 'A packet of biscuits?' he said, apologetically.

'That should do nicely.'

Padre Martin introduced 'Senor' Vazquez to the rest of the children. At least Emil assumed that was what was being done, as it was conveyed in the same impenetrable local patois. It could have been an instruction to prepare a cauldron of boiling water for all Emil knew.

He pondered that thought. The people of Ariloch might not have been cannibals, but they weren't far from savages, judging by the state of their offsprings' clothes and what they lived in. They even appeared to share the village's dilapidated accommodation with the chickens and goats he could see milling around. In fact, there didn't seem to be much evidence of a normal community at all. No vehicles to speak of, or any other kind of machinery for that matter.

Emil wondered what the villagers did to earn a crust. If they were farmers, then where were the horses, ploughs and carts? How did they till the land or tend livestock? The few animals Emil could see appeared more like pets.

The children Emil assumed to be from the orphanage drew nearer as the padre continued to allay their suspicions of the stranger, giving the policeman a chance to eye the potential witnesses more closely. Not that they would have been reliable in court.

Whatever their roots, years of inbreeding was much in evidence – mainly in and around the children's eyes which were either too close together, or too far apart. It gave many an almost frog-like appearance.

Some surgical work had been done to ease the plight, but although well intentioned, nearly all had been blighted further by the procedure. Some of the scars ran so deep, parts of the brain must have been removed in the process. Emil tried not to wince at the most severely disfigured.

There was no escaping the impression of a Victorian freak show. Emil was both disgusted and fascinated and couldn't take his eyes away. A morbidity replaced by pity again, however – along with some considerable guilt – when Emil's interest was rewarded with broad smiles.

The posse of youngsters returned – cradling one thing and dragging another. Pedro was dumped at Emil's feet before an argument began over who should be the one to hand the pistol back.

The young detective fretted as the weapon was pulled back and forth between the orphans. Padre Martin clapped his hands and they stopped. All the children bar one then groaned as the pastor uttered a few more unintelligible words and the next thing Emil knew, the smallest of the group took hold of the gun's barrel in one hand, the grip in the other and approached Emil. Beaming proudly, she raised the pistol like a peace offering.

Emil took the handgun, removed the magazine and pulled the top slide back to ensure the chamber was empty. The children recoiled in horror as if their Maker was about to strike them down. All except Pedro, who seemed in awe of the safety procedure.

Another clap of the hands made everyone turn to the padre. He was polite but firm. 'The children and I would be grateful if you could keep that well out of sight during your visit.'

Somewhat embarrassed, Emil released the slide, eased the hammer and placed the pistol back inside his jacket. He slipped the magazine into a pocket but not before pressing down on the top round to ensure they were all still there. Zipping the two halves of the jacket up to his neck, Emil forced a smile. It didn't seem to improve the Arilochian's negative concerns. The padre coughed towards the holdall.

'Oh yes, of course.' said Emil, falling to his knees. He rummaged through the bag, looks of horror turning back to curiosity as he did. Emil produced the biscuits and the eruption of excitement that caused stunned him. The reverend certainly had the orphans well-disciplined, for they calmed just as quickly.

Emil decided to give the packet to the little girl who had returned his handgun. She grinned before moving off to share the treat amongst her fellow playmates. All except for Pedro.

'He has to learn.' The pastor's Svengali-like grip of his backward community seemed to extend to some pretty rough justice. 'The carrot and the stick play an important part in Ariloch and Pedro knows that. Don't you, Pedro?'

The boy looked at the reverend and then at everyone enjoying the biscuits. He nodded before pulling his withered arm closer and getting up to move away.

Emil's compassion returned. Snatching the pistol had been wrong but he still wanted to help Pedro. Emil would like to help all of the children, but that was out of the question.

There was something about the boy's gait. 'How old is Pedro?'

'Seventeen.'

'*Seventeen?*'

'Well, I christened him that long ago, so unless my maths has let me down again.'

'But he seems so young.'

'If you don't believe me, you can always check his medical records.' The padre had extended a hand past Emil's shoulder.

Emil squinted at the setting sun. There was a hill with what appeared to be a large house silhouetted on top. The mention of clinical documentation reminded Emil of his task. 'I'd better take a look at the crime scene while it's still light.'

Padre Martin turned his head to one side. 'Crime scene?' The little girl approached the pastor with what was left of the biscuits and he knelt beside her. She offered him one of the last two in the packet. 'There's been no crime. We just want to report a missing person.'

Chapter 3

The Padre's comment both surprised and concerned Emil. 'What do you mean, "no crime?" What else do you call murder and abortion?'

The padre took one of the biscuits from the packet, broke it in two and gave one of the halves back to the little girl. She gave him a hug and the reverend stood back up.

'Same as you I should imagine. But I very much doubt anything so disturbing has happened in Ariloch in a long time.'

The child ran over to offer the detective the last biscuit. Emil approached the pastor instead. The little girl followed.

'I'm here to investigate infanticide. Are you saying there hasn't been a murder?' The little girl held the packet up again. Emil looked down at her and shook his head.

'Not to my knowledge,' said the padre. 'I'm sorry if you've had a wasted journey.'

Emil glanced at the house on the hill. 'I'll be the judge of that, Padre.' He set out for the property, grabbing his bag on the way. An entourage of children headed by the little girl followed.

The detective mumbled to himself. *'If that bastard Gomez has sent me on some wild goose chase just to get me out of the office so he can grab a week's worth of bribes to himself, I'll fucking kill him when I get back – RHIP my ass.'*

Emil thought about the return journey he would have to undertake. '*If* I get back.' He stopped, as did the children. The little girl tried again, but Emil continued to ignore her.

The padre caught up and Emil raised his latest fear. 'Are you certain there are no communists here?'

The reverend appeared puzzled. 'Absolutely. Like I said, there's nothing here for anybody.'

The contract killing of policemen wasn't unknown. Anyone with the right money and connections could have it done, especially with so many militias – government backed or not – out there with something to prove. But Emil was hardly a prime target. The detective had always been meticulous in his duties and especially when dealing with the darker side of it but the informers and other seedy types he plied for information relied equally on him for bungs in return and Emil had never reneged on those.

They didn't have the connections anyway, and even if Gomez had decided his newest sergeant couldn't be trusted after all, surely he wouldn't have Emil killed for it? And why in the middle of nowhere? If his boss were that desperate to get rid of him, he could do it himself down some dark alley and blame muggers. Emil tried ridding himself of the more fanciful conspiracy theories.

The building was beginning to take on the appearance of a haunted house as the sun set behind the mountains, so Emil increased the pace of his final steps, casting a detective's eye over the scene when he got there.

Although the European design wouldn't be conspicuous in some of the more affluent suburbs of Buenos Aires, the house stood out in Ariloch and especially the condition it was in – almost new compared to the neglected and ramshackled sheds passing as accommodation in the rest of the village. Even the church didn't look as well maintained. The garden had been neglected by comparison with the swings and roundabouts that once made up a playground much in disrepair. The children fought with each other to show off on them when they noticed his interest. All except one very determined little girl, whose arm now appeared permanently outstretched towards Emil.

He was about to refuse her again when the front door was opened from the inside. A young woman in her mid-twenties stood before Emil.

It struck him straight away how different she was from the others. The same genetic Pampas roots, mixed with southern European blood, but none of the children's physical abnormalities or medical complications were evident. Emil was wondering if that contrast extended to the young woman's mental health when the way she spoke seemed to answer that.

'Good afternoon, Mr Vazquez. Welcome to Uncle Joe's house.'

The polite delivery of her perfect Spanish made Emil realise something else. She was pretty too. For a peasant, of course.

Father Martin climbed the steps of the porch and stood next to her, as did the children.

'May I present Ariloch's most famous citizen? This is Senorita Maria Fierro.' The pretty young woman smiled which made Emil blush for some reason. The children giggled. 'And we're very proud of her – she's going to be a doctor one day.'

Maria scoffed at the padre's description and hopes, and stepped towards the police officer. 'I'm just an orderly at the local hospital.' She put out a hand to greet Emil. 'If you can call twenty miles away 'local'.'

Emil shook Maria's hand. But he couldn't shake the feeling something was wrong. A hospital orderly? In a house where abortions took place?

'What are you doing in this house, Miss Fierro?'

Maria glanced at her priest. 'Making sure it's clean and tidy in case Uncle Joe returns.' The padre corrected her.

'*When* he returns.' Maria didn't argue.

'Who's "Uncle Joe"?' said Emil.

Maria opened her mouth to speak, but the pastor interrupted. 'Only the saviour of these good people.' He raised his hands and looked up to the heavens. 'And when God sees fit to release the great man from whatever greater good his healing hands are required to do elsewhere, he shall return here to complete his work.' Two of the children moved next to the reverend. He smiled and placed a hand on each of their misshapen skulls.

Emil continued to question Maria. 'You commute to the hospital every day?' She laughed and the way her face lit up made Emil blush again.

'Of course not. It's much too far, but I try to come back to my birthplace as often as I can.' Maria looked down the hill towards the rest of the village. Her eyes seemed to mist over. 'Not that there's much to come back to in Ariloch these days.' She knelt and put her arms around the youngsters closest to her. 'Just the children.'

Emil thought the scene very strange – a tall, middle-aged priest and a pretty young woman surrounded by a litter of misshapen inbred children, all smiling at him. Emil firmed his determination.

'Show me the house.' Maria gave him a look. For some reason Emil thought he ought to add 'please' so he did. She smiled again and beckoned to enter.

The door opened into a hallway, lit naturally by a glass skylight from the floor above. The first of that night's stars could be seen so Emil flicked a light switch. Nothing happened.

'Would you like me to start the generator?' Despite his refusal to believe a crime had been committed, the reverend still seemed keen on assisting the police with their enquiries.

The visitor looked at his hosts. 'Is there mains electricity in the village?' Emil had guessed the answer to that halfway through saying it.

'No, but there's a telephone in the church.' Father Martin's departing reply suggested it was the only utility. All the children, bar one, followed the padre outside to where Emil assumed the house's power supply must be.

Recovering a torch from his bag, Emil cast a light, revealing pictures lining walls. He guessed Uncle Joe to be a first or second generation European as they were all landscapes from that part of the world. Scenes of the countryside, ornamental gardens and storm-hit coastlines predominated.

The housekeeper and the persistent little girl followed Emil into a reception room, the child taking hold of Maria's skirts as they did. The little girl was uncomfortable and Emil wondered why.

The European theme continued, with dark wood panel walls and furniture that plainly belonged to someone with not just taste but money and even status – the chairs were studded in burgundy leather, and heavy ashtrays lay on the occasional tables placed between. Emil stepped onto the room's plush carpet, and recalled the smoke-filled atmosphere of an ambassador's residence he had once waited on as a cadet. A carved marble mantelpiece dominated this room too and he pictured the mysterious uncle leaning on it with a glass of brandy in one hand and a cigar in the other, chuckling to himself over the money to be made from his sickening trade.

Emil looked at Maria. Surely, such a sweet girl couldn't be Uncle Joe's accomplice? He had only just met her, but it would crush what little faith Emil had in humanity if she was. Emil suppressed the thought by pretending to examine the expensive drapes framing the tall windows that overlooked the village. The contrast between the two worlds was quite staggering. The idea of some butcher enjoying this lavish lifestyle while the Arilochians struggled to survive just a hundred metres below, made Emil seethe. He was beginning to understand the communists' point of view.

Not that sympathy would do him any good if the Reds got their hands on him. The thought made Emil speed up his investigation. He opened one of two doors that led from the room into what turned out to be a short corridor before a kitchen.

Maria lit a candle as she and the little girl followed. The child began whimpering and clung on more to the housekeeper but she couldn't be consoled. There was something the little girl didn't like and her increasing concerns told Emil he was getting close to what it was – kitchens were where nearly all illegal abortions took place.

Like the reception room before, the kitchen was immaculate with the long table in the middle bearing evidence of having been scrubbed – it was still wet. Emil wondered what had taken place there. Copper pots, pans and other utensils hung at various points throughout and spotless crockery adorned extensive wooden shelves. The pretty housekeeper had ensured this room was ready for the owner's return, too.

Keeping an eye on the little girl's reactions, Emil began opening drawers, expecting an increase in her distress to give away the location of the tortuous tools he was looking for. Emil hated the idea, but if anything even remotely capable of tearing

19

a foetus out of a woman appeared, he would arrest Maria there and then – regardless of the 'uncle's' whereabouts.

As anticipated, the child became more agitated the further Emil progressed so he was somewhat surprised to find the last drawer empty. Emil scanned the four corners of the kitchen before biting his bottom lip in frustration. The kitchen's function appeared to be exactly that. He took hold of the door handle to the next room. It was locked.

The little girl let go of Maria, and screamed as she ran to Emil. The biscuit packet was still in her hand and he was about to lose his temper when the child wrapped her arms around Emil's legs and to his amazement, lifted him away – her strength for someone so young and small was remarkable. Floods of tears made the little girl's speech unintelligible, but it was clear she wanted Emil well away from whatever lay behind that door.

Putting the candle on the table, Maria rushed to prise the child from Emil. Her welcoming demeanour changed. 'We don't go in there.' She gave Emil a key. The child bawled into Maria's shoulder as the pair retreated back through the house.

The detective unlocked the door. Like the rest of the building, what lay beyond was dark with Emil's torch lighting the top steps of what must have led to a basement. Unlike the rest of the house however, dust was everywhere and Emil had to wipe cobwebs to get to a light switch. Expecting the generator to burst into life at any moment, he flicked the switch and began a descent.

Emil had only taken a couple of steps when it hit him – the smell. A faint but unmistakable mix of blood and disinfectant identical to the much stronger odour that pervades every pathology lab. Nothing could be seen, but there was no doubt in Emil's mind – this was where the atrocities had taken place. But when?

Not recently, the constant need to remove ancient spider works from his face told Emil it was a long time ago and probably years.

Emil paused to sweep the blackness with the flashlight when it occurred to him the uncomfortable but familiar scents masked a third. Something not immediately identifiable but just as foreboding. Not being able to see what lay ahead was both frustrating and fearful. Emil's heart raced with trepidation.

Continuing down, a step at a time, the torch illuminated the floor at the bottom. Emil traced the pool of light along its surface until the base of a cabinet appeared. He raised the beam up – senses now pitched perfectly to identify even the smallest of clues. Which was probably why the shock of what Emil saw next made him drop the torch.

Although dead, the contents of the glass jar appeared to scream the moment it was illuminated. The grotesque head of the creature inside even seemed to turn towards Emil as if wanting to convey the full horror of what it had suffered.

If it could be called a head. The flashlight had extinguished the moment it hit the floor but Emil's mind's eye continued to the see the disturbing details: oversized eyes, non-existent nose and ears, a mouth open so wide it seemed to detach the misshapen skull from the additional limbs and externally developed organs that was supposed to be a body. If this poor creature had been born naturally, it didn't live long.

Emil's battle to fight or flight had begun the moment he shocked himself into darkness and was about to be resolved when he heard the distant sound of a diesel engine being started. The lights came on.

Imminent panic was replaced by instant disbelief. The sudden brightness caused Emil to squint, but that did little to lessen the effect of what row upon row, and tier upon tier of identical glass jars had on him. He now realised what the third smell was – embalming fluid.

Every container had either an under or overdeveloped aborted foetus or stillborn child in various states of preservation. Why? Why keep them? The other illegal abortion clinics the police busted either flushed the results down the lavatory, used incineration or tossed the remnants into the nearest dust cart – they certainly didn't keep the evidence, let alone preserve it.

Emil made an estimate of their number – it ran into the hundreds when he realised the jars were stored at least two to three deep. There must have been more villagers on those shelves than in the local cemetery – the figure certainly exceeded those alive and like the living, their appearance both fascinated and repulsed. Emil forced himself away to investigate the rest of the basement.

Even to his untrained eyes Emil could see the cellar was more than well equipped for the relatively simple procedure of abortion. Although old and uncared for, the sophistication would put many a modern hospital to shame: a proper operating table with the correct lighting above, various electronic monitors, bottles of gas and masks for anaesthesia. The space even seemed to double as a laboratory – test tubes and similar glassware sat on the surrounding surfaces along with Bunsen burners and a microscope. Spotting a trolley of surgical instruments Emil pulled open the top drawer.

'Bingo,' he said out loud when what he'd been looking for turned up. Emil gave the other drawers a cursory glance before lifting the lid of an autoclave. It contained an electric drill.

Emil was thinking about what to bag and tag when his attention was drawn by what appeared to be a dentist's chair in the corner of the basement. It had some kind of frame attached to the back, giving the device the appearance of a reject from a ladies' hairdressing salon. The chair was on wheels so Emil pulled the device into the light for a better view.

As with a salon's hairdryer, the attached frame was meant to fit over a person's head. What had that got to do with abortion? He recalled the orphans' disfiguring scars.

The head frame had various guides, lugs and attachment points for surgical instruments. Narrow tubes extended uniformly out and around with clamps at the base that made it clear they were designed to slide down and come into contact with the wearer's skull. Curiosity piqued, Emil recovered the electric drill from the autoclave, returned to the chair and introduced the bit it contained. Other than complaining against a touch of rust, the drill bit passed perfectly through the tube Emil had selected.

He approached the macabre collection next and, wiping the film of neglect, peered into one of the glass jars. The head of what was inside hadn't been drilled but it bore the evidence of forced intrusion – the brain was exposed and in a state that even a layman like Emil could see was little short of butchery.

He chose another. It was the same. And another. Emil skipped a few levels with the intention of using random selection to confirm the preservations had all been similarly defiled but then realised the trauma was reducing in severity. It appeared more methodical. Calculated even. The exposed brains of the early jars progressed to holes in others, then less crudely designed access points to incisions that seemed almost delicate in the craniums of later specimens. The surgeon was finessing his skill.

But then something more than visually disturbing became apparent.

Along with the clumsiness of the early attempts, the physical appearance of each cadaver seemed to improve too. Not enough to be pleasing to the eye by any stretch of the imagination, but enough to show that whatever had been done to the brain, seemed to result in a physical change to at least one of the poor victim's features.

The jars weren't in any random order; their placement appeared to reflect increasing knowledge of not only how the brain worked, but how it could be manipulated to affect development. Emil looked at the chair and the attached head frame. It was clearly meant for much older 'specimens'. He wondered what the mysterious uncle had managed to achieve before he went missing.

Emil had no idea how, why or what had been done in the basement, but he doubted selfless altruism towards the people of Ariloch was behind it. Emil stood back and looked at the wall of dusty, web-covered specimen jars and the story of artificial creation they seemed to tell.

Maybe the orphans weren't inbred at all. Maybe they'd been made that way.

Chapter 4

Emil backed towards the basement steps and sat down. He lit a cigarette.

'Magnificent, aren't they?'

The sudden appearance of the padre caused Emil to drop the packet. He picked it up and spun round. 'Magnificent? You're joking, aren't you? This place is straight from a horror movie – *Frankenstein*!'

Padre Martin descended the steps, unable to take his eyes from the display. He seemed to be in an almost trance-like state.

'Oh no – Mary Shelley created a fictional monster that begat another fictional monster. Our Lord God in his infinite wisdom has once again seen fit to send us his son.' He looked at the detective. 'And as the good book foretells, Jesus has returned to raise the dead for all eternity.'

Emil took a step back. The padre's words had left him temporarily lost for any of his own. He regripped the reality that appeared to elude the pastor. 'Father, whatever has been done in this basement, *Jesus* had nothing to do with it.' He pointed at the hundreds of prematurely terminated lives. '*That* is pure evil.'

The padre regarded Emil as if he were naïve to the situation. 'Don't be deceived by their appearance, Sergeant.' He turned back towards what a Second Coming apparently results in. 'You and I would have been just as displeasing to the eye at their stage and we don't look too bad now, do we?'

The policeman put a hand to his brow as if trying to make sense of the statement. 'Are you saying those poor creatures are actually alive?!'

'Of course not, but they soon will be.' Emil was rendered speechless again. The padre seemed to sympathise with him. 'Forgive me. I know it's a lot to take in and as a committed Christian my passion can sometimes come across as overzealous, but what has happened here and will happen again is truly a miracle.' He genuinely appeared to believe the absent 'uncle' was God's son. 'And when Uncle Joe returns, he will lead us *all* into the kingdom of Heaven.'

The padre approached the chair and ran his fingers over the head cage-like device. 'Just as he did with Maria's brothers.'

For the first time, Emil picked up on something that could have some sense behind it – albeit just as disturbing. 'Brothers?'

'Oh yes.' Martin pushed one of the cage's tubes down through the frame. 'They're in the caring hands of Our Lord now.' He carved a sign of the cross in mid-air.

'Padre Martin? Where *are* Maria's brothers?' The padre closed his eyes to pray. Emil was in no mood for any spontaneous acts of faith no matter how important they were to the worshipper. 'I said: WHERE ARE THEY?'

'I've already told you, but I assume you're referring to their mortal remains.' The padre looked towards the top of the basement's steps. 'They're in the church. Their mother is keeping vigil over the coffins until I perform the funerals tomorrow.'

Emil threw what was left of the Marlboro onto the floor and

repacked his holdall. He went to retrieve the torch but the priest was holding it.

'Try not to interrupt *her* prayers, Sergeant – the forgiveness of sins is important.' He shone the flashlight in Emil's face. 'I wonder if anyone will be there to do the same for you when your time comes?' The torch was handed over.

Emil dusted himself down and got out of the house. He was about to head straight to the church when he realised Maria was waiting for him at the front door. At least that was the impression. The outside air temperature had fallen and Maria drew the coat she was wearing tighter around her.

'Don't you ever stop being a policeman?'

So much for the secrecy of 'Mr' Vazquez. Emil was about to say, 'no' but decided to commiserate first – no matter how false his stress might make it sound. 'I'm sorry for your loss, Miss Fierro.' The condolence had all the sincerity of a card sharp.

'I guess the answer to my question is, 'No'.' She turned on her heels and headed for the church.

Other than a campfire and feeble glow of the occasional candle through a window, the route was in darkness so Emil used the flashlight to guide their way. He sensed she didn't want him too near her, so walked a pace behind and to the left so the casting of her shadow didn't make the gesture pointless. It meant lighting only Maria's way which risked him stepping into something he'd rather not, but Emil wanted to make some kind of amends and given the circumstances, being unselfish with his torch was probably the only thing he could do. Appropriate or not, there was no escaping her rights might still have to be read.

They passed the campfire where some of the children could be seen making toast. They laughed and teased each other with the sticks used to keep the bread at arm's length. The picture couldn't have been more opposite to the horrors of the basement. Even the persistent little girl appeared to have got over her attempts to keep Emil out of it. A mangled packet could still be seen in her hand and Emil wondered if she might follow but guessed it was too dark to identify the torchbearer.

There were no adults present at the joyous scene, and it made Emil realise he'd yet to see any. In fact, other than the padre, Maria and her mother, Emil had yet to see, meet or even hear a mention of anyone above teenage years.

'Maria? Where are the adults? I know Pedro is seventeen, but that still makes him a minor so where are all the parents and grandparents?'

Maria stopped and turned to face him. She looked like an ex, annoyed at Emil for forgetting her birthday or something. Her arms were folded tight, but that was probably because of the cold. Emil wanted to put his arm around her.

'There aren't any. They gradually lost faith in Uncle Joe's return and began drifting away years ago. Only the orphans remain now and the church looks after them.' She continued her journey and Emil rushed to ensure the remainder of it was clear.

They entered the building. The interior was in darkness save for an abundance of candles and tea lights that surrounded the altar, and the short aisle that led up to it. Appropriate organ music could be heard and Emil wondered who must be playing when the sound wavered for a moment indicating the tape machine's batteries were running low.

He turned off the torch and accompanied Maria down the aisle. A woman in black knelt in front of six tiny coffins. Six!

Like other second and third world countries, large families weren't unusual in Argentina and especially in remote villages like Ariloch. Disease and malnutrition meant many children were unable to survive birth let alone the journey into adulthood, but six brothers of the same family and all at the same time? Only two things caused that kind of mortality and as the village didn't appear to be suffering from a pandemic...

Emil was wondering what the protocol was for accusing someone of murder during their prayers when his ribs took a jab from an elbow. He mimicked Maria and drew a sign of the cross on his chest. Anyone watching would think they'd been married for years. They took their place in a pew together just as naturally.

Like the majority of Argentinians, Emil was a Roman Catholic but hardly a regular churchgoer. He often took advantage of God's power to forgive, though – usually at the guilt he felt when taking bribes from families that couldn't afford it. The hours he'd spent in a confessional box far outweighed where he was seated now.

Maria's mother was deep in prayer. She had a set of rosary beads clasped between her palms and paused occasionally to stare at a statue of the Virgin while whispering her Hail Marys. She then looked at the coffins which Emil now realised were nothing of the sort – just wooden boxes. Their size meant the brothers couldn't have been much more than toddlers when they died which was strange because Mrs Fierro must have been well into her forties. He put it down to the hill farmers' ability to breed like rabbits.

Emil assumed her to be the 'village idiot' who'd murdered her 'sprogs' – Inspector Gomez plainly didn't think much of the country's less-fortunate citizens. Emil wondered if he could be just as judgmental. Of course not – Maria and her mother were like any other God-fearing family. For peasants of course.

But there was no escaping the law and questions needed answering. Emil checked his watch. The vigil could go on all night. He nudged Maria and the look she gave him more or less confirmed the possibility.

Emil was wondering how best to interrupt, when God seemed to do it for him – the tape player's batteries surrendered. The sudden silence caused both women to stop mid-prayer and look up. Emil seized the opportunity and approached the elder of the two.

'Please accept my condolences at such a difficult time, Mrs Fierro.' His ability to convey sympathy hadn't improved. 'I'm Sergeant Vazquez from the Buenos Aires police and I'm here to investiga—'

The woman sprang to her feet and clutched the front of his jacket. 'You've found him? You've found my boy? Please tell me you've found my son?!'

For a moment, Emil wondered if the shock of losing six off-spring had been too much for the mother when Maria separated them.

'No, Mama. We've only just reported him missing. The policeman is here to help us.'

Emil was even more confused now – he had assumed the missing person to be the strange 'uncle'. The village of Ariloch was beginning to turn into the proverbial riddle, mystery *and* enigma.

'Excuse my ignorance, Mrs Fierro but did you say your *son* is missing?' Emil turned to the coffins. 'But I thought—' He interrupted himself when the widow broke down. She rested her head on her daughter's shoulder and the tears flowed. Emil didn't know what to make of the look Maria gave him this time.

The door to the church opened and Padre Martin entered. He

was carrying something heavy and for a second Emil thought things were about to get yet more complicated with a *seventh* coffin, when he realised that it was, in reality, a truck battery. The padre placed it on the ground next to the tape machine.

After wiping his hands on his cassock, the padre approached the three. 'Take your mother up to the house, Maria. She's hardly eaten a thing in the past two days.' It was a straight-forward request and yet imparted in such a compassionate and caring way. Emil envied the reverend that ability – despite his disturbing comments earlier.

Maria encouraged her mother to leave and the door closed behind.

'What the hell's going on, Padre?'

The pastor grimaced before making another sign of the cross, closing his eyes and asking his Maker to, 'Forgive this misguided youth.' He opened them again. 'Nothing is *going on*, Sergeant. We regularly get storms which sometimes uncover graves and I'm afraid this time it's the turn of the Fierro family to suffer the pain of a reburial.'

His explanation was plausible. Most communities grew up around rivers or lakes and rising waters were well known for their destructive force – even whole cemeteries could be washed away. Emil once had the misfortune of witnessing the grisly detritus being removed from a storm drain. It wasn't exactly a joy for the workers who had to do it either – how they withstood not only recovering but untangling the putrid mess of bones and still rotting corpses was beyond him.

Emil pursued his line of questioning or more accurately, clarification. 'Is one of her sons missing?'

'Maria had seven brothers – septuplets to be precise, but only six of the boys have been found.'

31

Emil sighed at what was starting to become a farce. 'Father, the cemetery is only just outside and the valley below at least a mile away so the torrent of water could easily have carried the body down to it. Some farmer will probably find the remains when the fields are ploughed in the spring.'

'They weren't interred in the cemetery and the water only disturbed the shallow topsoil that covered them.' Padre Martin placed a hand on one of the coffins. 'Maria discovered her brothers' remains in the grounds of the house, and one is missing.'

Chapter 5

Emil looked at the coffins. Maria's brothers had almost certainly been murdered – the discovery of a shallow mass grave all but proved it, but by whose hand and why?

He studied one of the caskets. The small wooden box had been hastily constructed with gaps and knot-holes visible all over. Emil bent down and peered into one. The burning wick of an altar candle could be seen right through on the other side.

'Padre? When we were in the cellar, you referred to the boys' bodies as *remains*. What exactly is in these coffins?'

'Their bones.' The padre made it sound obvious. 'They have been in the ground for eleven years.'

That surprised Emil, but made sense considering the age and state of what was in the basement.

He recalled what he'd seen so far: the children, the specimen jars and the chair with the strange head-cage device attached. He stood back. 'I'm afraid I'm going to have to look inside each of them.'

The reverend made his way to where he'd placed the truck battery. He may have been God's representative and in charge of his house, but the legal obligations of a mortal man still held sway. The padre returned with a claw hammer and handed it over. 'Just remember where you are.' Emil was left to the grisly task.

The heel of the tool was inserted under one of the coffin's lids and the four nails holding it down gave way. The box contained a hessian sack secured at one end with twine. The size and shape told Emil it contained what he was expecting and he untied it. The sack gave off a strange, oily odour as he did.

The end of a paper refuse bag was revealed, but it was wet with the contents and tore when opened. Emil screwed his face at the mud-encrusted arm or leg bone that emerged.

The light of the candles meant detail couldn't be seen, but the bone's length in comparison to the coffin made one thing clear – the boy wasn't a toddler. Maybe as old as eight or even ten. A pathologist would be able to determine that through photographs and of the skull in particular. Gritting his teeth, Emil reached inside and searched but became frustrated when the familiar shape didn't come to hand. He reluctantly emptied the mess of mud and remains into the coffin. Emil then realised what the smell was – diesel fuel.

To begin with Emil thought the skull was missing with just the lower jaw present. He wiped away mud in preparation of the pictures, but noticed the jaw had suffered some kind of blunt-force trauma – all the teeth bar one had been removed and with such force that much of the supporting bone had given way too. Emil was in the process of placing it next to what he now realised was a thigh bone when he spotted the front of the skull.

Expecting the cranium to be behind, Emil prised it from the surrounding earth only to discover why he'd failed to identify the head in the first place – there wasn't one. Just the front of the skull with the upper jaw again showing signs of a determined effort to ensure any existing dental records couldn't be used to identify the child.

Emil wiped as much earth away as he could and grabbed his torch for a better view. Whoever had done this didn't only want to ensure identity would never be known, but what had been done surgically kept a secret too – the precisely drilled incisions the detective was expecting to see appeared impossible to confirm as the cranium had been destroyed in the same brutal way. Emil ran a finger over the sharp edges of what had survived before turning back to the pitiful debris of earth and skeleton that had once been a little boy.

It took a while, but fragments of the crown did eventually reveal themselves. Emil put each one next to the other remains he'd cleaned and kept going – he wanted to see how skilful the surgeon had become before departing the scene of his crime. The detective allowed himself a moment of satisfaction when what he was searching for, appeared.

The shard didn't show a complete hole, but it was enough. Emil took out a handkerchief and with the help of some spit, eked out the semi-circular evidence. He wiped his hands as best he could and retrieved a camera from the holdall.

The sombre organ recital restarted and the padre made his way back. He drew a sign of the cross on his chest when he saw what Emil had done.

'So, have you finally decided to accept the inevitable end of our mortal selves, Sergeant?'

Emil attached a macro lens to the camera and zoomed in tight on where he thought the pathologist would be most interested. 'Well, I'll tell you what I've found so far, Father and let you decide.'

Emil continued to gather his evidence while explaining the facts. 'The specimens in the basement have undergone some kind of pre or postnatal brain operation that appears to have affected their growth. The children still alive seem to have suffered the same and now we have the bones of six boys found in a shallow grave in the grounds of where your so-called *miracle* took place.'

He put down the camera and picked up the drilled fragment. 'This bears the same evidence, and I'm willing to bet the other remains will too.' Emil regarded the pastor as if to judge him. 'And just in case what happened in Ariloch eleven years ago still isn't clear to you, the skull was deliberately smashed to try and hide the perpetrator's handiwork and a smell of diesel tells me the bodies were probably burned for the same reason.'

Emil provoked him. 'So what do *you* think, Father? Try to help me understand why *Jesus* decided he not only had the divine right to terminate the lives of unborn babies but the existence of six healthy little boys too?'

The padre was unmoved. 'Ashes to ashes, dust to dust, Sergeant. They are all with our Lord God in Heaven now which is how it should be.' He approached the altar and knelt to pray.

Emil lost his temper. 'Now listen to me, Padre. The only reason I don't arrest you right now is because I don't believe you're capable of killing anybody let alone these boys, but I'm not stupid.' He pulled the preacher's hands apart. 'Who are you protecting and why?'

The priest wrestled away and stood. 'To paraphrase something not in the good book, *there are more things in Heaven and Earth, and you and I cannot possibly hope to understand them.*' His spit flew. 'Did Noah question why the Ark had to be built or Abraham the need to move his family to Canaan?' Martin prodded his lost sheep in the chest. 'You have much to learn, Emil – even Moses who'd led an entire nation out of slavery found the door to the Promised Land barred to him and all because he dared to question the word of God.' A quote from Isaiah followed, *'Behold, the day of the Lord comes, cruel, with wrath and fierce anger, to make the land a desolation and to destroy its sinners from it.'*

A series of similar passages from the Old Testament were reeled off as if to prove something, but Emil didn't hear them. He was thinking about two other people who would have been around at the time of the murders and one in particular. His fledgling feelings for her were starting to cloud his judgment.

Emil needed a distraction and anyway, the discovery of the boys' remains and their connection with someone long since departed was above his pay grade now. It was time to pass the whole sorry affair up the chain.

The priest was in the middle of *fire and brimstone* when Emil interrupted. 'Where's the telephone, Padre?' The still angry host didn't halt his diatribe but did point to the rear of the church.

Emil entered the office, grabbed the receiver and asked the operator for a connection to his precinct. Gomez snatched the phone from whoever had answered. He was his usual mix of brusque, no-nonsense authority and sarcasm which he liked to think was a sense of humour.

'Have you done as instructed, Sergeant? Or am I going to have to redistribute your bonus to a good cause elsewhere?' Laughter in the background just seemed to encourage Emil's boss. Gomez eventually allowed him to speak.

Emil was just getting into the sickening works of the village's very own *Doctor Moreau* when to his disappointment, the inspector announced some difficulty with the line and he would have to call him back. Gomez then put his phone down. Emil thought he heard another receiver being replaced before doing the same

37

at his end.

The only phone for miles rang as expected and Emil's natural suspicions were confirmed when he heard the unmistakable sound of a third telephone receiver being lifted from its cradle. He was about to warn his boss with the appropriate code word when it became clear the only thing Emil would be required to say during the one-sided conversation was, 'Yes, sir' at the end of it.

'Now, listen to me, Sergeant. I gave you strict instructions to ensure everything is buried. I don't give a fuck if it's one, six or six hundred bodies, you're to ensure *all* of them and *all their belongings* are buried. Have I made myself clear?'

Chapter 6

Emil put down the receiver, and tried coming to terms with what he was required to do. Surely that didn't include the orphans? No, of course not – by 'bodies' Inspector Gomez meant those no longer living, but he didn't just mean the remains of the brothers – it was clear the victims in the basement had to be interred too.

'Belongings' didn't require much imagination either – everything connected had to go, but why? Emil was basically being told to dispose of evidence against a murderer. The inspector's integrity as a policeman might have been as grubby as Emil's own, but no detective in his right mind would turn down the chance of bringing someone so monstrous to justice. Unless...

The padre entered the office. 'It's getting late. You need to finish whatever it is you're doing.'

Emil stood up. 'I have what's required, Padre, and will put everything back as found, but there's something I need to check in the house first. Is the generator still running?'

The reverend nodded before looking at the six coffins and the undignified state of one in particular. 'I'll finish up here. You do what you have to.' He turned back to the officer. 'I took each one of them out of the ground with my bare hands, anyway.'

Emil's opinion of the padre mellowed at the thought of what

that must have entailed.

Grabbing his bag, Emil walked out of the church and began making his way back up to the house. The campfire had died down, but there was enough of a glow for him to see Maria had joined the children still sitting around it. The boisterous antics of before had been replaced by what looked to be rapt attention of a bedtime story. Emil decided to stop and listen to Maria's words and soon became just as captivated. *'She would make a wonderful mother,'* he thought to himself.

Emil didn't intend to but found himself sitting on a log next to Maria just as the final words of the fairy tale were read out.

'... And the prince and the princess lived happily ever after.'

Maria and Emil stared at each other and the children giggled. Emil started to say something genuine for a change when a certain little girl put what was in her hand between the pair.

Maria's eyes widened at Emil as if any honourable intentions he had towards her rested on his very next decision. He smiled at the child before finally accepting the packet. The little girl grinned back and clasped her hands together in keen anticipation. All the children did.

Aware the jury might still be out, Emil unwound the packet and tipped as little of the crushed biscuit as he could into the palm of his hand. He made sure the child saw him pop the crumbs he selected into his mouth before giving the majority of the treat back to her. The little girl whooped with joy, performed a short victory dance and then hugged them both before running off.

Her pleasure affected Emil. 'I can't get over how happy and well-behaved the children are.'

'We have Uncle Joe to thank for that.'

Emil regarded Maria as if she were as mad as the padre appeared to be. 'How can you say that? He placed a hand on her arm. 'Maria, you do know your brothers were murdered?'

She sobbed. The children fretted as if waiting for Emil to do the right thing. They relaxed again as his arm went around her waist. Maria dropped her head to his shoulder and the youngsters regained their smiles too.

'I don't understand it. He was always so kind and generous to us all.' Maria tilted her head up. 'Why would he do something so awful?'

Emil didn't know if it was the tears or the close proximity of her lips, but it just seemed natural to place his lips against them, so he did.

The children erupted into a frenzy of joy and began smothering the new love birds with kisses of their own. It took a good few minutes for the adults to calm them which ended in groans for some as Maria announced it was way past their bedtime. She took hold of two tiny hands and the rest followed behind. After a few steps, Maria hesitated and turned back to Emil.

'Are you going up to the house?' Emil nodded. 'Mama's asleep in one of the bedrooms.' She gave him another of her looks. 'Don't wake her.'

'I only need to go into the study, anyway.'

Maria appeared to think for a second. 'You won't find anything.' She herded her kittens and they continued on their way. Emil surveyed the retreating scene and wondered if Maria and he would have children of their own one day.

Emil picked up his bag and a few minutes later, opened the front door to the house. The lights were still on and the reassuring hum of the generator could be heard in the background.

Turning left from the hallway, Emil found the study. It was just as elegant and clean as the rest of the house above ground and doubled as a library. As could be expected, the books that lined the walls contained surgical or medical text with what he presumed to be some of the owner's own handwritten and sketched manuscripts. The detective couldn't hope to understand what it all meant, but it was plain some serious research and development had gone into whatever the murderer was trying to achieve – or had achieved.

In searching for the killer's identity, Emil found the drawings dealing with the design and operation of the head-cage device, but it was a strange cradle to grave depiction that intrigued him most. No wonder Padre Martin was convinced of a Second Coming – the hand-drawn graphics appeared to show some kind of provable link between man and God. What had been done to the specimens and the children was detailed too, along with an explanation of the science behind a method of *visiting* Heaven. There was even a Raphael-like depiction of the divine creator at the top of each page.

Emil was starting to understand how a devout man like the padre could be taken in by it all. It must have come as quite a shock when the brothers' remains were found and in such an irreverent state – certainly out of context with what Emil was looking at now. Not that the specimens in the basement were much better off, but they hadn't been baptised which in the eyes of the Church made them little more than pickled eggs.

But that was all academic now. He had his instructions and would carry them out to the letter – as soon as his curiosity of the author's identity had been satisfied. He opened one of the drawers to the desk. It was empty. He tried another. That was empty too. Emil went through the rest but other than the occasional item of stationery all were void. He tackled a filing cabinet of medical records next, but that proved just as fruitless.

Emil was about to start on the rest of the books when he heard a noise from behind. Instinct made Emil withdraw his pistol.

'Is this what you're looking for?' Maria held out a small booklet.

Emil put the gun away and took the passport which he soon realised would never allow international passage, even if it was still in date. The front cover confirmed what he had begun to suspect but refused to believe the moment he saw what was in the basement. Emil opened the official document and stared at the bearer's picture. He'd seen it many times. He checked the name. Emil had seen and heard that many times, too.

The police were already looking for the notorious Nazi – as was the rest of the world.

Chapter 7

'You do know who this is and what it probably means?'

Maria nodded. She looked guilty, even though there was no need. 'Are you going to arrest me?'

Emil shook his head. 'It's all now well beyond what I was sent here to do. I have new orders and they don't involve taking anyone into custody.' He picked up some of the anthropological-like sketches the doctor had left behind. 'What I don't understand is why he wanted all of this preserving? Having said that, there's enough evidence in his own country to send him to the gallows.'

Maria took one of the drawings from Emil. 'He didn't. He left strict instructions for it to be destroyed if he didn't return within a month. It was the Church that ordered it to be kept ready, regardless.' She pointed at the sophisticated graphics. 'You can see why. Uncle Joe was close to finding a way to not just go to Heaven but return from it too. I think the Church hoped proof of the hereafter could be used to restore faith in those who'd lost or didn't have it in the first place.'

Emil peered at her. 'And you believe that nonsense?'

'I did when I was younger, but not now. Not now I've seen what he did to my brothers.' She put her head down and Emil stood up to comfort her.

'It's okay. Everything's okay. We'll find the monster and bring him to justice, I promise you.' The detective may have had a good handle on the law's priorities, but he still had a lot to learn when it came to understanding women's. Maria pushed him away.

'I don't give a damn whether you find him or not – I want my brother back! What are you going to do about it?' Their new relationship appeared to have settled into a familiar routine already.

Emil's shoulders sagged. He knew there was about as much chance of finding her sibling as he had of making chief of police. Same old story. No money and even fewer resources, not to mention the luck required to secure what would undoubtedly result in a seventh coffin anyway. He cared enough about Maria to show willingness, though. 'Do you have a photograph?'

Maria reached into her apron and produced a family portrait. Although over a decade had passed since it was taken, she and her mother stood out, but not so much the septuplets. Their father was absent and a ragged edge to one side suggested he'd been deliberately torn from the photograph. *Guess I might not have to ask for permission to marry her, then*, Emil said to himself.

He was about to enquire after her father when something about the brothers made Emil pursue a different question. 'How old are you in this picture, Maria?'

'Fourteen.'

Emil switched on a desk lamp and retrieved the magnifying glass he'd spotted in one of the drawers earlier.

The photograph was a professional studio portrait, but its underdeveloped nature told Emil it was one of the trial and error prints made prior to the final copy. The washed-out appearance meant much of the detail had been lost, but one thing was

45

evident – the boys were the same height as their sister.

Emil thought the remains he'd studied in the church might have made the boy as much as ten, but a teenager? He passed the magnifying glass over the memento in the hope of solving the mystery when a framed version of the exact same image was placed in front of him. Maria's mother stood back and folded her arms.

It was the final print approved and the clearer detail led Emil to an unexpected revelation.

The reason why Maria and her mother could be made out in the first picture was because of their skin and hair. Along with the man still attached to this version of the scene, both were much darker than the boys. No wonder the septuplets could barely be made out in Maria's copy – they were white with blond hair. There was no doubt in Emil's mind, had the print been in colour their eyes would probably have been blue.

Maria's mother's roots were Pampas and her father's southern European, but the boys' own origins lay well north of both continents – maybe even as far as Scandinavia. It would explain why they were so tall for their age. Emil concluded they had been adopted.

Mrs Fierro must have seen the policeman's judgmental look many times before – she turned on him. 'I carried my boys for nine months and nearly died giving birth to them!'

Maria came to her mother's defence. 'It's true. I was only eight, but I can remember Uncle Joe delivering them like it was yesterday.'

Emil started to fear for his sanity. 'Eight? That makes the boys *six* in this picture!' They were only a few inches shorter than the man in it.

The septuplets weren't just identical – their growth and

angelic appearance were unusual too. They couldn't have been more opposite to the children Emil had seen so far – alive or otherwise.

The picture that had begun developing in the detective's mind ever since he first set foot in Ariloch began revealing its details too. Emil went through the evil eugenicist's manuscripts again. 'Mrs Fierro. May I ask how you became pregnant with the boys?'

'It's called, in vitro fertilisation.' The three of them jumped at the padre's sudden appearance. Maria's mother went to him and he put his arm around her. Martin used his free hand to pick up one of the sketches. 'Uncle Joe really was the saviour of this village you know. He arrived here not long after the end of the war when the people were desperate for relief from a conflict of their own – against nature.'

The padre pulled up a chair and sat Maria's mother down. 'There are only so many crop failures and livestock diseases a community can withstand before it gives up all hope and Uncle Joe arrived with the one thing everyone including the Church needed – money. Each time God saw fit to punish the people for their sins, Uncle Joe brought in fresh stock and told the villagers they'd been forgiven. Throw in the blessing of healing the sick and you can see why the village would do anything for him.' The implication of the padre's next statement didn't appear to concern him in the least. 'Including the offering of women and children for his work.' He passed Emil a sketch detailing the process required to impregnate a surrogate mother with pre-fertilised ovum.

Like the other drawings, it too had a depiction of the Holy Father at the top that implied it came with some kind of divine approval. The reverend echoed that sentiment. 'God's work.'

The picture in Emil's mind became complete. The Nazi

eugenicist hadn't just continued his evil experiments after escaping what should have been his fate in Germany – he'd finished them in this tiny South American village some twenty years later and by using its people as human guinea pigs. Lab rats needed to refine what the monster had always planned for the embryos he brought with him. Even six of those were callously murdered once the job was done – the creation of just one *perfect* child. A boy.

A boy the notorious Angel of Death took with him when he left.

Chapter 8

Emil lit a cigarette. 'I'm sorry, but I've been given strict instructions to destroy all of this.' The three of them looked at each other before nodding in unison.

Emil was concerned the pastor's somewhat misguided commitment to God might interfere with the process. 'You do understand that means *everything*, Padre?'

'Yes, I understand. I received a telephone call instructing me to assist you.'

'Telephone call? Did my inspector speak to you, too?'

'No, the bishop.'

Emil had suspected a higher organisation lay behind Gomez's almost desperate demands for the evidence to be destroyed and assumed it to be the government when he saw the passport, but the Church's involvement and in such a rapid way implied a level of national interest bordering on the hysterical.

Emil needed to test his host's apparent change of heart. 'Padre, will you help me carry these manuscripts down to the campfire?'

The pastor seemed preoccupied but otherwise willing enough. 'Yes, of course.'

The detective extinguished the Marlboro and the four gathered as many of the documents as they could. Emil kept an eye on the pastor as they descended the hill. He was compliant but plainly troubled by whatever the bishop had said.

They reached the deserted campfire and soon had the paperwork reduced to ash. The pastor made no complaint or excuse throughout so Emil assumed he would still be on board when it came to executing the main part of the plan – burning the house to the ground. Emil put it to him there and then.

There appeared to be no issues with that either. The pastor stared at the full moon silhouetting the cross on the church while making a suggestion. 'It might be best to do it straight after the funerals tomorrow. You'll need somewhere to sleep tonight anyway.' Everyone agreed.

The bed was comfortable, but Emil was plagued by nightmares.

The infamous doctor and his unspeakable experiments featured, and animated visions of the most grotesque tormented Emil throughout. Although every imaginable horror was presented, the twisted surgeon's figment also appeared to taunt with some kind of purgatory that lay in wait for those deemed less worthy of his attention.

Emil feared what the madman would do if Maria made an appearance and when she did, tried everything he could to protect her – all to no avail of course. But then something even more horrifying happened.

Instead of being just as fearful, Maria seized the doctor with both hands and forced him into the chair instead. The look on the twisted medic's face indicated it was the last thing he was expecting, but it was Maria's expression that shocked Emil more as she then rammed the head-cage down, picked up an electric drill and began boring into the doctor's skull.

Emil could see this was no mere act of revenge – Maria was enjoying the experience and the maniacal expression she maintained throughout told the young policeman he was going to be next. Sure enough, once Maria had removed everything she needed from the doctor's brain, the body was unceremoniously tipped into a vat of formaldehyde. The scene was so vivid, Emil could smell the chemical's pungent odour.

As anticipated, Maria reached for him next and, despite his feelings for her, Emil fought against the vision.

'Get up, Emil!'

There was no way Emil was getting into that chair and he thrashed his arms. Maria's mother appeared and grabbed him too.

'Emil, wake up!'

His body was being shaken by the force of their combined strength.

'Emil, wake up – Father Martin's in the basement!'

He sat bolt upright. The smell of embalming fluid in the air was unmistakable. Both women were upset but of the two, Maria's mother the most hysterical.

'He said he had to baptise the children and I thought he meant those in the village, but that can't be right because they've already been—'

Emil cut her off as his half-awake mind realised the serious-ness of the situation. He shot out of bed, ran downstairs in his underwear but only to choke on fumes. Emil shouted back upstairs for the women to grab their things and get out of the house as soon as possible. Emil burst into the kitchen – the door to the basement was open.

'Padre Martin, get the hell out of there!' No answer.

A sound of breaking glass made Emil grab a cloth to cover his face.

Halfway down the steps, the pastor could be seen – shattering every one of the doctor's macabre collection with a hammer. The contents then received a prayer and a sprinkle of holy water from a flask. The putrid mess that slopped across the floor made the atmosphere almost impossible to bear.

Emil dropped the cloth from his face. 'Padre, you *must* get out. The fumes are highly flammable. The slightest spark and the place will go up like a bomb!'

The pastor stopped. 'Isn't that what you want?' He stared at the sea of dead and decaying flesh. 'Isn't this what *God* wants?' He returned to the containers still intact on the shelves. 'Get yourself and the women away from here, Sergeant Vazquez.'

Emil put the cloth back to his face and took a deep breath through the material. He ran down the last few steps, determined to do whatever it took to get the reverend away from certain danger. The last jar was broken, the remaining contents of the flask emptied, and the final Hail Mary uttered just as Emil reached the bottom. The pastor took out a box of matches making Emil stop.

The matchbox was opened. 'This is all my fault. I stood back, let the Devil wreak havoc and did nothing.' The pastor looked at the stunned policeman. 'Pray for me, my friend.' He struck a match.

The basement had no windows or other doors, so the only release for the blast was up the steps. Emil went with the pressure wave. He shot out at the top, across the kitchen floor and clouted his head against the wall at the far end. The heat searing Emil's skin dissipated as the blast was sucked back by the vacuum created, but a dazed Emil then watched in horror as flames began spreading out from the basement once more. A plentiful supply of formaldehyde vapour encouraged the consumption of everything in its path.

Emil shook his head and tried to stand, but increasing heat forced him to stay crouched. He found the door and scrambled through both it and the rest of the house as fast as he could, lungs desperate for fresh air. The failed rescuer reached the front door just as the flames caught up and assisted Emil's escape – by ejecting him out of the house like the unwanted guest he was.

Emil staggered down the path where Maria and her mother helped pull him to safety. They and the children then began a series of half-hugs and inspections to ensure he was still intact.

It took a couple of minutes for Emil to realise how lucky he'd been before like the rest, watching the house burn to the ground.

A funeral pyre for those forgotten by God but remembered by Father Martin.

Chapter 9

They stood in silence beside the graves. No one knew what to say.

Padre Martin had done what was required – the dead and all their belongings were buried.

Emil's eyes wandered over the graveyard. Despite the village having so few inhabitants, it was unsettling to see the brothers weren't the only children recently interred. Juvenile funerals were a regular feature judging by the many areas of disturbed earth and the unweathered wooden crosses marking them. There were even freshly dug graves and size made it plain they weren't intended for adults. Earth lay piled to one side as if ready to be shovelled back in at a moment's notice.

Maria's mother broke the silence. 'They need flowers.' The children took that as an instruction and headed off with her into the woods to find some. Emil noticed his little stalker wasn't amongst the group. He glanced around. She didn't seem to be anywhere.

The object of his affections looked at the smoke rising from the top of the hill. 'What will you do now?'

'Head back to the city I suppose.' Emil took her hand. 'What about you?' He paused before adding, 'us?'

Maria ran her fingers through his. 'Do you really think a

relationship between a city boy like you and a country girl like me could work?'

She had made it sound romantic, but Emil knew what Maria meant. Their two worlds weren't just distant geographically; the couple were poles apart culturally too. His new love may have been part Spanish, but that still made her an *indio* to some and even though his southern European heritage was just as 'corrupt' with North African ancestry, their visible difference wouldn't go unnoticed and especially in the country's capital – racism was as endemic in Argentina as corruption in its police. Emil knew being a third-generation immigrant from the wrong part of the world meant he would never make chief of police but by marrying Maria he could say goodbye to inspector too.

Emil dismissed the fears. 'We'll make it work. I'll find a way.'

Maria made it obvious she wanted to kiss him and he bent down to oblige. She studied his face afterwards. 'I've decided naivety is your most attractive feature.'

Emil narrowed his lips and was about to protest when a hand was placed over his mouth. 'I have to be here for the children. Write to me at the hospital and don't be a stranger.'

Emil wanted their relationship to mean a lot more than that and was about to explain it when shouting made both look up.

'Maria! Senor! Come quick!' It was Pedro. They ran to him.

The teenager was standing next to one of the dwellings that appeared to double as animal shelters. As if to emphasise that, a couple of chickens shot out when Emil and Maria stooped to enter.

The interior of the accommodation couldn't have been more opposite to what Emil was expecting and it surprised him. The open space was laid out like any other child's bedroom – only it was the tidiest he'd seen. Clean and well organised, the few toys it contained were placed more like trophies than forms of entertainment. A hessian mat lay in the middle of a swept floor and a tiny child-sized wooden chair sat next to an equally small table which held a cardboard dolls' house that had seen better days. It was arranged as if to show off to any visitor how its owner hoped to live one day. Emil's attention fell on her.

Curled up like a foetus, the little girl lay motionless in the cot-like bed. Emil placed the back of his hand against her cheek. It was cold. Tiny hands could be seen above the blanket that covered the body and Emil began weeping the moment he saw what was still in them.

From initial pity on arrival to growing disquiet with his investigation, to the horror of the basement, to his utter disbelief at the final exposure of the truth, all the emotions Emil had thus far managed to suppress came tumbling forth at the sight of an empty cellophane wrapper. He fell to his knees.

'I didn't even know your name.' The thoughtless oversight seemed to complete his feelings of hopeless inadequacy.

Maria was just as moved, but the almost weekly occurrence made her better able to cope with yet another premature end to an innocent life. She drew a sign of the cross before putting a hand on Emil's shoulder. 'Her name was Sofia.'

Emil took out a handkerchief to dry his tears but ended up wiping them away from Sofia's tiny misshapen head instead.

He regained his composure. 'I'm going to find your brother, Maria.' Wrapping Sofia in her blanket, Emil lifted the body. 'And the monster that did this. And when I do, I'm going to kill him.'

Chapter 10

Emil drifted back down the track. He couldn't remember a time when he'd felt so dejected. Other than meeting the girl of his dreams, there wasn't one single positive aspect of his visit to Ariloch. Even Maria's reciprocated feelings were tempered by a frustrating but admirable duty towards the orphans, not to mention her 'cultural' concerns.

She was right of course. If their relationship were to survive, it would need to be conducted away from his judgmental boss and colleagues, but that meant a visit whenever he had leave and three days of that would be spent travelling. What serious relationship survives on being together just a couple of weeks a year? Emil didn't know but he sure as hell was going to give it a try.

He choked at the thought of Sofia. Without a padre, Emil couldn't even attend her funeral. The best he could manage was the construction of a wooden box within which he laid Sofia's body along with some of her toys. Emil left the wrapper in Sofia's hands. It didn't seem right to remove it somehow. Maria had ensured the Church was aware and a new padre would be sent but in the meantime, she and her mother would attend a vigil of the little girl's coffin – along with the remaining orphans' needs. Emil wondered how long it would take for all the children to succumb to the evil they'd suffered.

His heart sank further at the pointlessness of it all. Even the telephone call he'd made to the inspector just before leaving couldn't snap him out of it. Gomez had appeared pleased enough, but the concern he expressed for his sergeant's safe return was a little over the top, even for him: 'Be careful when you're on your own, Emil. Be *very* careful.'

Emil stopped. Having travelled up just the day before, he knew how exposed the track was and anyone watching would have known a return journey all but inevitable. Emil put down his bag and extracted a map to see if there was an alternative route.

He'd only just opened it when the sound of footsteps behind Emil made him take out his gun. Emil expressed a sigh of relief when he saw who it was. As ever, Pedro's eyes darted between the Browning and its owner.

Emil was about to reholster the weapon when it hit him – the chance to salvage something *positive* from his visit.

Had anyone from the Church been present they would have no doubt disapproved of the idea – along with Maria and her mother – but if anything, that would make the moment that much sweeter. Emil didn't care if handing back fewer rounds of ammunition than signed for would cause questions and he certainly didn't care if his boss found out. No, Emil was going to make one mischievously curious orphan's day – maybe even his life; Emil was going to let Pedro fire a gun.

The rusting carcass of an old car lay nearby. The policeman cocked his pistol, released the safety and put a bullet through the windshield. Pedro's mouth dropped open at the shock of both cartridge and glass exploding. The smoking weapon was then offered and the way Pedro ran towards it made Emil feel better already, but he wasn't stupid – the gun was hoisted out of reach and a pair of handcuffs presented instead. If anything, the teenager appeared more excited at the prospect of being 'arrested'.

Pedro grinned and lifted his withered arm. Emil secured his own wrist first and then his eager pupil's. There would be no repeat of what had happened the day before.

Keeping the pistol pointing towards the old Ford, the boy's just as enthusiastic instructor encouraged him to take a firm hold. Pedro wrapped his hand around the grip – which was all the opportunity he needed.

Within less than a second, the gun had not only been snatched from Emil yet again but the handcuffs slipped too. The stunned policeman prepared to pursue another fruitless chase when to his sickening horror, Pedro stood his ground and pointed the gun – straight at Emil's chest.

Had Emil had time to think, he maybe would have pondered his murder as a fitting end to an investigation that seemed to consist of nothing but death. Even its style would be appropriate – his killer, with probably less than a year to live and nothing to live for, would, at least, be able to challenge St Peter with something, anything to avenge the evil of what had been done to him. What had been done to him and all the other children by a seemingly kindly man from a land far away.

Emil closed his eyes and tried not to blame anyone, but himself. Not even his boss. A boss who had warned him to be extra vigilant only an hour before. Emil never thought he'd make inspector anyway. He whispered goodbye to Maria just as two shots rang out.

Emil opened his eyes to see what Death looked like. Pedro lowered the gun. Something made Emil spin round. It was the final breaths of two men lying dead on the ground.

Emil searched his thumping chest as if expecting to find holes in it, but the position of the bodies indicated the two projectiles had passed harmlessly either side. Pedro crept up to Emil, as if not knowing if what he'd done was a good or a bad thing. Emil retrieved his gun before making sure the boy knew it was most definitely the former – the weapons still in the would-be assassins hands attested to that.

Pedro was beside himself with joy. It was as if he had finally done something that didn't result in a hiding, humiliation or exclusion. Something that ended in what he'd always wanted but never received – a hug. Like Sofia the night before, the boy whooped and performed a dance which ended in a hug for Emil too and then a run back to the village as fast as his little legs could carry him; to tell the rest of the children no doubt. Not that they would believe him. Emil didn't think they would swallow his version of events back at the station either. Pulse still well above normal, the policeman put himself back on duty and approached the bodies as any other homicide officer would.

The shot through the Ford's windscreen must have made the pair break cover from their ambush. It was clearly a put-up job. Light clothing and stylish leather jackets meant these two weren't part of some rag-tag communist militia prepared to lie in wait for days on the off-chance – they were professional hit men.

Emil didn't expect to find any identification but was about to search the bodies anyway when he recognised the type of weapon each had planned to kill him with – a standard police-issue Browning nine-millimetre. The air's temperature appeared to plummet and Emil shivered. He reached inside the jackets hoping not to find what he did – their warrant cards.

Emil's eyes wandered back up the track to where the police

officers' executioner could be seen, running. Pedro turned and waved. Emil was in shock but he waved back. The loose end of the handcuffs dangled and Emil looked to see how the slippery eel had managed to escape so easily.

It was quite simple really. Pedro used his good hand to tear through the high-tensile steel.

Chapter 11

Inspector Gomez opened the door to his office and switched on the light. He had stared down enough gun barrels in his career not to be too fazed by what was being pointed at him. The sight of a sergeant sitting at his desk was a different matter, however.

'Get the fuck out of my chair.'

'Give me one good reason why I shouldn't kill you right now.'

Thirty years of dealing with desperate men holding guns told the seasoned officer his dishevelled junior was serious, but Gomez still thought it worth giving seniority one last try.

'I said, get the fuck out of my chair before I walk over there, take that pistol out of your hand and beat some sense into you with it.' Gomez wondered when the duty desk officer would notice his raised voice. It shouldn't be long – it was six in the morning and the place as quiet as the grave.

Emil stood up and extended his aim. He threw what was in his other hand onto the desk. 'Why did you send them to kill me?'

The inspector didn't need to look at the warrant cards. The bodies had been found two days earlier. Gomez regarded Emil in a way he never thought he would. 'Did you kill them?'

'No. The person who released themselves from these did.' Emil threw the useless handcuffs on top of the police IDs. 'But my own people want me dead and I want to know why.'

The tension in the older man eased at the relief his sergeant wasn't a cop-killer but also because the query implied at least a chance of surviving the current encounter. Gomez looked at the rent and twisted metal. Where the hell was that idiot of a desk officer?

'I didn't send them.' said Gomez. 'I was told to ensure any bodies found in Ariloch were buried – that's all. I assumed some criminal gang with connections had paid to have their tracks covered.'

Emil lowered his gun a little. 'Who told you?'

Gomez glanced over his shoulder as music from the local radio station began playing. The desk officer was in for the beating of his life – assuming his boss still had his to dish it out, of course. Gomez refocused on Emil. 'I receive my orders in the same way you do – the next rank up.'

Emil sat back down and motioned for his superior to do the same. Emil kept the Browning pointing at Gomez. 'If you didn't send them, then whoever was listening in on our telephone conversations, did.'

Gomez was determined to exert some control over the situation. 'Do you think I don't know that? The second you opened your mouth about the basement, I knew two things: what I'd sent you to do was much more than a routine cover-up job and your life was in great danger and not from some Marxist gang.' He picked up what was left of the handcuffs and gestured with them. 'Whatever's going on is well above our pay grade – why the hell do you think I told you to watch your back?' The gun was lowered a little more.

Emil reached inside his jacket and passed Gomez a photocopy of a passport.

Like his junior, learning what was in the basement had

made Gomez realise that one of the world's most wanted men was probably the man responsible. Seeing his official picture confirmed it. 'Where's the original?'

'Somewhere safe. I want you to tell the captain that if anything untoward should happen to me, you or anyone else then it will immediately be made public.' Applying the Browning's safety, Emil offered the gun. Gomez took it. 'And that includes the paperwork detailing the involvement of Church and state. I shouldn't think the world would be very impressed to discover this country not only supported but continues to protect the Nazi to this day.'

* * *

It was all nonsense of course. The passport was certainly safe but not in the hands of anyone with connections to a *free* press – that was just as sewn-up by the junta as everything else. The evil doctor's manuscripts didn't exist anymore either. No, Emil was trying to protect his life and that of anyone he knew with the bluff of the century. It didn't impress Gomez who used the gun to hit Emil as hard as he could.

'Now get the fuck out of my office!'

Dragging himself from the floor, Emil put a hand to his chin. It was wet. Gomez stood to one side and after following his junior, walked to the duty officer, struck him in the face with Emil's pistol too, and ended *Baker Street* by smashing the radio onto the floor and putting a foot through it.

'Just in case anyone else is in doubt as to who's in charge around here.'

Gomez returned to his office but before entering, paused to slam Emil's gun down in front of him.

'And the next time you decide to take on the big boys I suggest you look in your desk first to see if your boss hasn't already second-guessed what his idiot of a junior police sergeant probably has planned given he survived one assassination attempt and is desperate not to experience another.' Gomez entered his office and turned round. 'Now go home and get cleaned up – you stink!' The door was slammed shut.

Emil looked at his gun, the blood on his handkerchief and the stunned expression on the desk corporal's face. Emil went through his desk.

The first thing he found was the envelope which Emil assumed contained the bribe payments promised – or rather the 'fair' share expected. Awkwardness joined his physical discomfort when Emil realised Gomez had been true to his word. The payments amounted to far more than Emil could have achieved on his own. He made himself feel better by assuming it was Gomez's way of assuaging his own guilt at putting Emil through the whole nightmare in the first place. But then Emil opened the desk's largest drawer.

The packet sealed with brown paper was so thick it couldn't possibly have fitted anywhere else. Emil estimated how much it must have contained. Gomez, the old fox. If you're going to make the bluff of the century then you may as well dress it up for the occasion.

The packet must have contained at least a year's salary and as much as Emil would love to splash out on a new car or holiday, there was no guarantee he would live long enough to enjoy either. Emil had to think of his future with Maria, anyway, so found a pen to write her address before forwarding it on. The packet was torn and Emil about to reseal the paper when what had become exposed made him stop.

Emil looked at the front desk. The corporal was licking his wounds so Emil tore the paper some more.

The estimated cash the packet contained increased ten-fold. It was the currency – US dollar bills.

1979

Chapter 12

The old man leaned on the gate and closed his eyes. He'd only walked a few paces. He didn't look like the perpetrator of some of the world's worst atrocities. Decades on the run from justice would seem to have taken their toll – scant compensation for his evil acts of course. Emil gripped the gun harder.

It had taken two years to find him. A task that had put Emil's own health at risk – Auschwitz's infamous 'Angel of Death' was being protected at every level and although the cost of penetrating that shield had been covered by the 'negotiated' payments, every dollar of it aroused unwanted interest somewhere and staying ahead of that had been crucial – including a distance from his boss. Never mind having to take an assassin's bullet, Gomez would do more than just punch Emil if he knew where he was.

Emil wondered what Maria was doing now. Their love had continued to build and was stronger than ever but seeing each other for just a couple of days each month was beginning to take its toll. He'd looked into getting a transfer, but as much as love conquers all, they both agreed careers should come first. The good news was there would soon be enough money to make a reality of Padre Martin's hopes for her. Institutionalised racism meant Maria having to attend a medical school in the United

States but Emil would be immensely proud if she did become a doctor. He tried not to think of what the far greater distance could mean for their relationship.

But there were more immediate concerns and Emil remained as determined as ever to avenge the murder of her brothers and the rest of the orphans. Out of the original thirty-two children, just Pedro remained. The steady supply of money had helped pay for their needs but there was little that could be done medically and even though the new padre did his spiritual best, one by one, the orphans succumbed to the evil doctor's crimes. It was like witnessing some kind of enforced extinction.

Pedro would soon go the same way of course. Even though the boy was now a man, he still appeared no more than ten-years-old and would welcome Emil to the village just as excitedly as the moment he realised he'd saved the policeman's life. But Pedro tired quickly now and his days of being able to bound over brooks and fences like a monkey or pull the trigger of a gun let alone break open a set of handcuffs were long gone. Emil had tried to get him to repeat the feat but even at his fittest, Pedro didn't seem able to understand the question let alone demonstrate it again. Maria said she suspected most of the children had possessed the skill but rarely exercised it and only when stressed – Sofia lifting Emil away from the door to the basement being an example.

But the vile perpetrator was now in front of Emil, and he expected the answer to that and many other questions were about to be revealed. Right before conducting some brain surgery of his own – using an unregistered nine-millimetre pistol.

Once the monster's lair had been found, Emil conducted the operation like any other stake-out and now had enough of the routine understood – the Nazi would pause at his front door to ensure no one had followed before checking again by looking out of the window and then, a few minutes after that, taking a seat in the back yard to smoke a cigarette and read a newspaper. He clearly had no idea what was about to happen to him – his eyes were shut most of the time. Emil couldn't explain it, but he had a strange feeling of being watched whenever that happened.

He opened a map to check his escape route. The former farm was far enough away from its nearest neighbour for screams not to be heard but two or three rounds from the Browning would be a different matter. The remoteness made witnesses unlikely but any person seen running afterwards would attract attention, so no matter what, Emil would force himself to walk the mile or so to where he'd parked the car with the false plates, ditching the gun *en route*. He refolded the map, checked his watch, and headed towards the rear of the building.

The sight and smell of cigarette smoke rising from the back-yard reassured him. Emil ducked down behind the wall that surrounded it just as a stomach ache began. He cursed the untimely onset and crept up to the ungated access. He took a chance his quarry would be engrossed in a news item and poked his head through the entrance for a better view. Emil was in luck – not only was the butcher reading his newspaper, but he had it open with both hands, obscuring sight of everything else.

Emil was about to take advantage of this good fortune when without warning, the cramps increased and with such ferocity he had to drop the gun to grab his stomach. If that didn't end any chance of catching his prey unawares, a spontaneous cry of agony must have done. Emil fell to the ground, cursing.

The pain was coming through in waves and in between Emil tried to recover the gun – the level of agony increased. He withdrew his outstretched arm and the cramps reduced. Emil looked to see what advantage his target had taken of the situation but to his amazement, the doctor not only hadn't moved but appeared to be still engrossed in the newspaper!

Pain became discomfort again, and Emil felt well enough to stand. A corner of the newspaper fluttered in the wind but otherwise didn't move. How strange. Emil decided to approach the apparently deaf reader. He pulled the top of the broadsheet down only to realise why the Nazi hadn't responded – he was dead.

Not only dead but just expired. The cigarette in his mouth was still burning, he didn't appear to be breathing and his eyes were closed. Emil felt for a pulse. He couldn't find one but the flesh on the body's arm was still warm. He had quite literally just died. There was no doubt about it, the look on the face was identical to that of the policeman's two would-be-assassins from a couple of years back – devoid of all life.

Emil sat down in a chair opposite, stomach still complaining. Talk about mixed emotions. He felt everything: relief, disappointment, shock. Even a frustrating sense of being cheated out of his form of justice. Emil pondered what to do next.

The door to the kitchen was open so he could try searching the house for the answers he, and what was left of the Fierro family, were after. It was a long shot but there was nothing better to do and certainly no need to rush – even if someone turned up, a lack of bullet holes in the body meant he could probably bluff or bribe his way out. Emil looked at the gun still lying in the dirt as another wave of abdominal agony began. He needed to get rid of that weapon in case it incriminated him. The pain subsided again.

Hot ash from the Marlboro was about to drop onto the newspaper, so Emil removed both from the cadaver's possession, stubbed out the cigarette in an ashtray and folded the broadsheet down next to it. He then lit his own smoke before setting out in the direction of some woods nearby. Pain resumed as soon as the gun was back in his hand but subsided as he walked. Before long, he was out of sight and scraping a hole in the forest floor. Pistol buried, he wandered back.

Emil's thoughts returned to Maria on the way. He had a strange feeling she would be both sad and pleased at the passing of her not-so-favourite uncle, especially without a shot having been fired, but disappointed if her love returned without knowing which one of her brothers had survived. Or if he was even alive. He would be nineteen now if he were – Pedro's age. That would be the only thing they would have in common, though. Emil took out the framed picture Maria's mother had demanded the doctor be tormented with. No chance of that now. Not that a monster like him would have been moved by it. Emil reached the entrance to the yard again and looked up from the portrait. The cigarette fell from his lips. Someone had placed the newspaper back in the body's hands. The joker had even lit it another smoke!

Emil glanced around and instinctively put his hand to where the pistol once was. He was about to run and retrieve it from the woods when the top half of the paper was folded down.

'I'm sorry – I must have fallen asleep. I'm always doing that. Thank you for saving my newspaper, I'm surprised I haven't set fire to myself in the past.'

Chapter 13

'But, you were *dead*. I checked your pulse.'

'I'm afraid that mistake often gets made with someone so close to dying of old age.' Doctor Mengele smiled. 'Don't worry. You're not the first and certainly not the most qualified to get it wrong – there's been many an embarrassed medic or disappointed pathologist before now.'

The monster finished folding his newspaper and placed it back on the table. 'It wasn't so long ago people were inadvertently being buried alive. Grave robbers often opened coffins bearing evidence of where the occupant had tried clawing their way out. Add the blood that must have been spilled during that to the apparent lengthening of nails and teeth by decomposition and it's easy to see where the vampire myth came from.' Mengele stood up. 'But then we humans have always had difficulty telling fact from fiction.'

Being faced with an evil far greater than Bram Stoker could ever have imagined made Emil make two fists but the return of cramps forced him to grab his stomach again. The pains eased once more. 'I know what a body looks like, Mengele, especially one that died just seconds before and you were dead.' An onset of nausea made Emil sit down.

'Mengele. Now there's a name I haven't heard in a long time.

I've used so many aliases since first coming to South America I've lost track of who I really am.' He sat back down next to his visitor. 'I believe you know me as 'Uncle Joe'.'

Emil was still being distracted by discomfort but picked up on what the doctor had said. 'How do you know that?'

'Just a feeling.'

The policeman-turned-vigilante wanted to get on with his questions but the pain refused to go. He put the framed portrait in front of his enemy instead.

Mengele studied it. He placed a hand on the glass and became sad. 'Maria.'

Emil's pain evaporated. He looked at the doctor – he was in tears.

If Emil's emotions had been mixed before, they were completely at odds now. It was like looking at a different person – an old man with a lifetime of regrets that an image had made too much to bear. Maybe that's what it was. Like an empty biscuit wrapper that had once tipped Emil over the edge, maybe a simple photograph was all it took for a monster to see the horror of its actions.

Mengele bowed his head. 'How are Maria and her mother?'

Emil's stomach ache returned. Strange. The doctor's head was scarred – the psychopath had actually operated on himself. 'You'll be pleased to hear they're still suffering from their loss, thanks to you.'

Mengele's lips tightened. 'I'm afraid you won't find me a very apologetic Nazi and if you're looking for an acceptable answer to my actions then you're going to leave disappointed.' He gazed towards the woods. 'Whatever you decide to do.'

Emil couldn't take his hands off his belly. 'I expected you to be completely unrepentant, Mengele, and I'm not here to listen to excuses, but how could anyone carry out such evil?'

'It's all relative, Sergeant. Some people would be just as shocked at your blatant abuse of families desperate to find their loved ones. I wonder what Maria would have to say if she knew the man she intends to marry extorts money from the weak and vulnerable?'

Emil ignored how Mengele could possibly have known that and snapped at him. 'That's completely different. Taking bribes doesn't involve the physical torture and murder of children – don't even think about comparing the two.'

The Nazi didn't let up. 'So the fact many Argentinians turn to suicide or starve to death through the poverty you cause doesn't bother you? And what about *the disappeared* themselves? I suppose your involvement in that particular genocide is just as acceptable.'

Emil lost his temper. 'How the junta runs this country has nothing to do with me; I just do my duty. The fact it results in thousands of deaths is just an unfortunate but sad necessit—' He became quiet.

'You and I are not so different, Sergeant. We *both* did or do our duty. It's only outsiders who fail to understand the necessity of having to kill an entire race of people to make the world a better place. As long as the perpetrators remain capable of writing the history books, nobody would even know let alone care.' He leaned towards the younger man. 'Have you thought about how *you* might have to escape the country of *your birth* should this particular military dictatorship fall?'

Emil stared at the ground. He'd always had a low opinion of his fellow man but thought himself basically good. He now realised he was no different to anybody else. Like beauty, the difference between good and evil appeared to be in the eye of the beholder.

'Of course, there's little difference between your president and the Fuhrer too. Hitler was just as impatient. I and many others often tried to get him to understand the long-term benefits of the carrot as well as the stick but he always chose brawn over brain. He really was the bloodthirsty tyrant the history books paint him to be, you know.'

Emil's physical pain reduced just as his emotional discomfort increased. He got back to the purpose of his mission. 'What were you doing in Ariloch, Mengele?'

The German beamed. 'Continuing my research into the eradication of war.'

Chapter 14

Emil grabbed him by the lapels. 'Now listen to me, you old fuck. The whole world knows about the horrific experiments you carried out on children at Auschwitz so if you're now saying that was done to end wa—'

Emil suddenly realised he was gripping his *own* neck tightly. The doctor was still sitting a few feet away – his eyes were closed but the position of his hands made it clear what was going on. Emil could only just get the words out. '*Let me go!*'

Involuntary strangulation instantly became a wilful massage. Mengele had put a hand to his own neck as if he too, needed time to recover.

Emil couldn't stop coughing. 'How did you do that?'

It was a while before he got a response, and a fatalistic one at that. 'Go and retrieve your gun, Sergeant. Finish what you came here to do.'

Emil controlled his fit and thought about recovering the pistol. The idea wasn't accompanied by pain. He looked back at the doctor. 'Not before you tell me what you were doing in Ariloch.'

Mengele glared at his would-be assassin. 'What's the point? You'll only get upset again, and I'd rather not die tired of trying to fight you off.'

The still angry but now intrigued young man would have

to control his temper if he were to get the answers he came for. Despite his revulsion, Emil had to listen and learn from everything this man had to say. Mengele had clearly achieved a good deal more than just superhuman strength in Ariloch.

Pedro's handiwork was placed on the table.

Mengele had recovered enough to inspect them. 'Which one of the children did this?' Emil told him.

The doctor put the useless handcuffs back down. He studied the family portrait again before lifting his head towards the fields and woods beyond. 'Why do you think we're here, Sergeant?'

Emil groaned inside. If he were to get what he came for, it looked as if he was going to have to suffer an old man's ramblings first. Emil decided to humour him. 'I don't know – to be happy?'

'Ah! Happiness – the ultimate goal which for some reason we spend most of our lives struggling to achieve.' He turned to the frustrated listener. 'Don't you find it interesting that *all* life on this planet spends most of its time struggling?'

Emil didn't bother answering.

'In nature, the struggle for survival is life's only purpose. It has to be. The Earth might be beautiful but it's far from a comfortable place. An uncertain climate, limited food resources and predators alone keep most living things on their toes.' He pointed towards a weed growing through a crack in the paving. 'I could concrete over that plant again and again but it would still try and fight its way to the surface.' A visiting bird tussled with a worm making its own appearance through the hardened cement. 'Wild animals are the same. Everything they do involves struggling to survive and usually just long enough to produce offspring.'

Mengele seemed to think he knew the meaning of life. 'And up until a hundred thousand years ago we were no different. But then along came our ability to make life easier – language, writing and then the printed word, the agricultural and industrial revolutions – all of which apparently came with a need to break the human race up from the hunter gatherers we once were into those that understood these new inventions and those that were required to work them.'

He turned his attention back to Emil. 'Which meant the knowledgeable became the masters and the ignorant their slaves.'

Under different circumstances Emil might have found it interesting but he wasn't there to philosophise. 'Get to the point, Mengele.'

'Well, aren't you intrigued to know why man's ability to make life easier is the reason why we go to war in the first place?'

Emil shrugged at what he thought was obvious. 'I guess it's got something to do with all those pissed-off slaves.'

'Actually, far from it. Keeping them under control was the easy bit and still is – just use their ignorance to create a culture of fear and dependency. That's why religion was invented. No one's going to obey another human being forever no matter how clever, but an invisible and all-seeing entity with the power over one's destiny? Now that's a different matter.' He regarded Emil as an atheist would a believer. 'As long as people think struggling through life as an obedient slave will eventually be rewarded, one person can control millions.'

Emil ignored the implied insult to his beliefs. 'So why are we always either at war or hell-bent on starting one?'

'Because life is not meant to be easy for anyone let alone a privileged few. A hundred thousand years of human invention cannot supplant a billion years of life struggling to survive and that instinct is so powerful, even when one of nature's creatures no longer needs to, it will *find a reason* to struggle.'

The bird won the battle and flew away with its prize. 'That thrush is no doubt off to feed its young which it would fight to the death to protect if it had to.' Mengele pointed at Emil as if it was somehow all his fault. 'And that is man's problem – making life easier should mean there's no need to fight for anything. But an instinct a billion years old says we should.' He settled back into his seat again. 'The trouble is, thanks to inventions like the hydrogen bomb, killing people has never been *easier*.'

Emil acknowledged Mengele's take on the madness of war but still wasn't interested. 'What has all that got to do with Ariloch?'

The old man hesitated before answering. 'If man's instinct for survival could be removed then all wars would end – it's as simple as that.'

Emil frowned. 'I'm no expert, but won't removing our instinct for survival just cause us all to give up and die?'

Mengele glanced towards his kitchen. 'Would you care for a cup of coffee?'

Chapter 15

Helping the world's most wanted Nazi into his house was the last thing Emil expected to have to do. Mengele clutched at his chest on the way in and Emil began to worry if the old man would even live long enough to unburden his evil.

The doctor fell rather than sat into a chair. 'My apologies – would you mind making the coffee? Black, no sugar.'

Emil cast an eye over the kitchen. Quite a contrast to what Mengele had left behind in Ariloch. The lack of Maria's touch aside, an abundance of polished copper pots above an immaculate cast-iron range were now just two tatty aluminium pans on a greasy stove. Even the water was questionable judging by the jerry can of it on the floor. Emil separated the two halves of a percolator and emptied the grounds.

'Bit of a comedown, eh? I suppose you're wondering where all the money went?' Mengele offered a cigarette and lighter. Emil took the latter.

'I'm more interested in where it came *from*.' He lit the gas.

The doctor placed the cigarette down on the table and drew another. 'There's no money in abortion, Sergeant – illegal or otherwise. It was the spoils of war that allowed me to continue my research.' Mengele put the cigarette between his lips and waited. Emil paused before lighting it. 'But it didn't take my hosts long to realise Nazis possess something far more valuable than mere art or treasure.' His chest appeared to swell with pride as well as smoke. 'A proven ability to turn a humiliated country into a proud and powerful nation interested them far more.'

A fit of coughing interrupted the hubris but not the history lesson. 'And the world would soon need a *new* superpower.' Emil was puzzled. Mengele elaborated. 'Once Russia had demonstrated their own atomic weapon, nuclear war with North America seemed inevitable.' The doctor dug out two cups and placed them on the table. 'As South America would have been one of the few continents still standing afterwards, an opportunity to lead the world into a new beginning seemed obvious.'

'So what went wrong?' The percolator started bubbling. 'Or right I'm happy to say.'

'What still exists to this day – the *deterrent* of nuclear war.'

Emil was still perplexed. 'But that was over thirty years ago and even if the rest of the world was wiped out tomorrow, Argentina's in no position to take advantage. Why didn't Peron or the junta just get bored and hand you over to the Israelis?'

Mengele seemed to have an answer for everything. 'They did. That's how the likes of Eichmann and others were caught – by the government either turning a blind eye or actually assisting the Nazi hunters. If it wasn't for the Americans, Mossad would have got to me too.'

Emil knew he was being deliberately drawn away from his original intent but the Nazi's words were still nonetheless intriguing. And anyway, given the world's level of interest in the monster, it was probably only right someone should be able to recount his last words.

The coffee maker fell silent. Emil removed it from the stove and filled the cups. 'Americans?'

Mengele's pride made a return. 'It wasn't just Argentina's steel and mining industries that needed to join the twentieth century, the existing agriculture was just as inefficient so I used my knowledge of embryology to set about improving the country's beef exports.' Emil passed Mengele a cup. Both his hands were needed to steady it. 'And when the Americans found out cattle didn't just survive the harshest of winters but went on to produce the highest milk and beef yields they wanted to know how that was being done.' He took a sip. 'Needless to say, when they found out who was doing it, they became interested for other reasons.'

'Bullshit! I don't believe it. You're one of the world's most wanted men. If the Americans had found you, they'd have given you straight to the Israelis. It's as simple as that.'

Mengele groaned. 'We've already been through this, Sergeant. There is no such thing as good *or* evil.' He made to end the argument. 'Over a hundred thousand Jews died constructing the V2 rockets that killed a similar number of Londoners during the Blitz, and yet both countries applauded the rocket's designer when he helped put a man on the Moon.' He became cynical. 'Don't you find it strange the Israelis have never even asked let alone *demanded* the Americans repatriate Wernher Von Braun to answer for *his* war crimes?' Emil didn't respond. 'It's thanks to loyal Nazis like him, that what were once little more than big fireworks have become today's sophisticated intercontinental ballistic missiles, capable of killing millions.'

Mengele put down the cup and stubbed out what was left of his cigarette. 'So, is it really that much of a surprise to learn the Americans would also want sophisticated *men* capable of killing millions?'

Chapter 16

Emil picked up the cigarette he'd been offered and lit it. He inhaled deeply while taking in the disturbing logic of Mengele's story. 'The *Americans* are protecting you.'

Mengele didn't respond.

The visitor looked at his host. 'But I didn't see anything *sophisticated* in Ariloch – cattle or otherwise. Just dead and tortured children.'

'Tortured? I appreciate you're no human rights activist, Sergeant. But tell me, just how upset and distressed were the orphans?'

It dawned on the young detective distress was the last thing the children appeared to be suffering from. If anything, they seemed unusually content with their lives – right up until the premature ending of it. The look on Emil's face answered the question. The old man got up to refill his cup.

'I know it's difficult, Sergeant, but try to see past the visually abhorrent and towards what was actually achieved – the creation of some very happy individuals.' He sat down.

Emil glared at the instigator of everything he'd been shocked by in Ariloch. 'You forgot *obedient*.'

Mengele's demeanour didn't change. 'The Americans' requirements were very specific – stronger, faster and *compliant.*

What's the point of building a nation of supermen only for them to take over what they were made to defend?'

Emil was disgusted. 'I always knew the Americans were no better than the Nazis.'

'No better than other *human beings*, Sergeant. Try to remember what a hundred thousand years of evolution have turned us all into: masters and their *slaves*. Guess which group you and I belong to?' Emil became quiet again. 'If it makes you feel any better, the Americans have been just as busy experimenting on their *own* people.' Mengele lit another Marlboro while reeling off a list: 'State-sanctioned sterilisation of the insane; the testing of biological and chemical weapons on the unaware; deliberate exposure to radiation and venereal diseases – take your pick.' He became thoughtful. 'Their own pitiful attempts to produce a *pure* race of people aside, the Americans would make excellent Nazis. They're just as determined to stamp their own authority on the planet but infinitely subtler about it. Their propaganda machine is particularly effective – countries that displease them aren't invaded, they're *liberated*. Conversely, freedom fighters that rise up against a tyrannical ally are considered *terrorists* and because Uncle Sam controls most of the world's media, nobody makes a serious attempt to question anything they do.' Mengele stared into space. 'I particularly admire the way *democracy* is used as an excuse to kill thousands of people in order to *free* them. He slowly shook his head. 'Pure genius.'

Mengele's cigarettes weren't lasting long, and he put the latest one out in an ashtray. 'Which is why their disinterest in my ability to create a race of super *masters*, surprised me.'

Emil glanced at the portrait. The seven lighter faces in it became more meaningful. 'You mean Maria's brothers?'

'There's a reason why Pedro was the most non-compliant of the children – he was the last to prove the potential of not just superior strength and endurance but enhanced reasoning and thinking too.'

The policeman recalled his near-death experience. Handcuffs aside, he had always wondered how Pedro had managed to dispatch the assassins so efficiently. The question of the boy's physical appearance was about to be answered too. 'Did you deliberately stunt the orphans' growth?'

'I don't think the government – Peronist, fascist or otherwise would appreciate having twenty or so not just super strong but super intelligent men and women wandering about the countryside.'

Emil broadened the unsettling scenario. 'I should imagine that would be *every* country's nightmare.'

Mengele lit his fourth cigarette. 'Actually, no. There was one forward-thinking nation – Great Britain.'

Chapter 17

'*Britain?* What have they got to do with Argentina?' Emil considered his own question. 'Other than getting kicked out of the Malvinas once the generals have stopped sabre-rattling.'

'The old lion might not be what it was, but they're still a force to be reckoned with. There's a good reason why most modern armies have adopted the English model. You might be surprised at how far they would be prepared to go to maintain sovereignty over the Falkland Islands.'

'But the British Empire is dead – there's no way they'd travel 8,000 miles to defend something they don't care about anymore. The world has moved on. And theirs especially.'

Mengele presented Emil with his empty cup. He got up to make a fresh brew.

'Their empire isn't dead – it's dying. Which is why the British were more interested in my work's potential to prolong life rather than end it as violently as possible.'

'*Prolong* life? Is that what happens once you've finished killing and enslaving a third of the world?' Emil didn't bother hiding his contempt for that nation too.

'Of course. It's just another example of nature's constant need to struggle and what happens when that's no longer required.' The doctor indicated through the open door. 'What happens to plants once they've finished growing?'

The recharged percolator was placed back onto the stove. Emil looked at the various weeds and untended flora in the yard outside. 'They go to seed and die.'

'Exactly. And like every empire or old country before them, Britain has gone to seed and is now dying.' He leaned forward in his seat. 'And just like South America is mainly made up of Spain's children, North America is the offspring of Great Britain.' Emil chuckled at the ridiculous analogy.

Mengele stood his ground. 'Empires, nations, states, countries – call them what you will, they all begin and end like most of nature's creations: they're born, they grow up, pick fights with the kid next door, grow up a bit more, find someone to share their life with and then have offspring keen to find *their* way in the world.' He sat back. 'Everything eventually grows old and dies, and like the rest of Europe, Britain and Spain are living out their final days.' He took another puff of his cigarette. North and South America on the other hand, are still very much in their belligerent and ideological early twenties.'

Emil challenged the hypothesis. 'So what happened to that young upstart, *Nazi* Germany?'

The doctor shrugged. 'He bullied too many old European mothers and fathers, who asked their younger American cousins to help and they did – just as any son or daughter would do. It didn't stop the US from thinking they're the rightful heirs to the throne of the world, though if anything, winning the war reconfirmed the entitlement.'

'Do you think America would come to Britain's aid again if we were to take the Malvinas back?'

'They might do but their inheritance concerns them more and all three countries are involved in fighting the greatest threat to it – communism. I don't think they would want to jeopardise that.' Emil passed him a fresh cup of coffee. Mengele offered what he thought would be the most likely outcome. 'Like many old people determined not to show it, I think Britain would fight to retain the islands but they'd much rather persuade you to leave.'

Emil looked through the back door and towards the woods. 'Like you *persuaded* me to bury the gun?' Mengele turned his head in the same direction but didn't reply.

Emil regarded the indentations on the doctor's head and recalled the device that must have been used to create them. He shuddered and reached for his cigarettes.

'How's it done?'

The old man coughed again and got up from the chair. 'Wait here.' He went into the room next door. Emil followed him anyway.

Unsurprisingly, the main living area was just as unkempt and basic as what passed for a kitchen. No wing-backed leather suites, marble fireplaces or medical libraries doubling as studies here – just sticks of furniture amid piles of old newspapers. Mengele went through some of them. A grunt of satisfaction accompanied the rediscovery of the edition he was searching for. The shock of seeing Emil peering at him as he turned around made Mengele clutch at his chest again. 'I told you to wait in the kitchen! Here, read that.' He thrust the newspaper at him before pushing past.

Emil was disappointed. After seeing the elaborate collection of handwritten manuscripts and drawings in Ariloch, the very least he was expecting was some kind of abridged version – not a tatty old tabloid with an item ringed in ink.

'*Doctors and priests hailed a miracle yesterday after mother of six,*

90

Senora Mirta Careaga, heroically rescued all of her children when their car overturned and caught fire. Incredibly, the forty-two-year-old not only managed to escape the inferno but actually lifted the vehicle off one of her children, before rescuing them all by wrenching open the doors of the twisted and burning sedan. Amazingly, only one of the family suffered any serious injury and all are expected to make a full recovery. Mama Careaga put the incredible strength needed to lift two tonnes down to healthy living and a strong belief in God.'

Emil re-entered the kitchen and placed the newspaper down on the table. 'So, you found a way to unleash superhuman strength. How does that become superhuman thought?'

The doctor tapped a finger on the news item. 'Nature's struggle for survival in action. Millions of years of evolution haven't just developed the more obvious strengths to assist that, there are hidden potentials in all of us that only reveal themselves under extreme circumstances. I made it possible for them to be used at any time.'

Mengele's pride reappeared. 'Although I'd proven the genetics required to increase the size and yield of cattle, the same studies would still be needed in humans so the Americans identified a village vulnerable enough to require not just a doctor but the resources necessary to function as a community too.'

'You mean the replacement of livestock and grain?'

Mengele nodded. 'The expectation being the villagers would willingly submit to even the most unsettling of my experiments if they also relied on me for their very existence.'

Emil's bile rose, but he had to keep it in check if he were to get to all of the truth. He offered one of his own cigarettes. Mengele's hands shook as he took it.

'But there was a problem. The Arilochians were deeply

91

religious and even though they could be bribed to turn a blind eye to the women I artificially impregnated and then performed abortions on, the foetuses I let survive to full term were deemed to be God's *miracles* – no matter how abnormal the results.'

Mengele's speech was wavering. He must have known he would soon be dead. Emil supposed anyone in that situation would find it difficult to talk.

'The villagers had to be convinced to allow their children to be sacrificed for my work and then one day the solution presented itself.' He became silent for a moment as if having second thoughts on what to divulge. 'My early experiments had been successful enough for me to chance repeating them on an adult. The villagers may have restricted my access to children but not grown men too disabled to work the fields and when I surgically altered the backward brain of one of them, what I was anticipating happened – he became both physically *and* mentally stronger.'

'And that made the villagers trust you again?'

'No, he never left the basement. Not alive anyway.' Emil's disgust was becoming harder to control. 'Once I realised his cognitive abilities had improved I set about exploring the extent of them but when he began answering questions that hadn't even been asked...' The doctor wrung his hands as he recalled something that must have been as traumatic for him as it was for his victim. 'He couldn't just read my thoughts, he could actually explore what was in my mind and I sensed every moment of it.'

'So that's how you know so much about me. You've been reading *my* thoughts ever since I first arrived.'

The eugenicist looked towards the front of the house. 'The range is limited and it becomes harder to discern between minds when others are present. That's why I left the city – the noise created by millions of thoughts became too much for me to bear.'

Emil was keen to know the extent of the new capabilities. 'But there's a big difference between reading a mind and persuading it to do something, Mengele. How did you make me think I was in pain or to ditch the gun?'

The question seemed to be ignored. 'Once the subject realised I didn't just abort foetuses, he fought against me, both physically *and* mentally.' The doctor looked into the back yard again. 'I was saved by what came to your rescue an hour ago – fatigue. Old age in your case but in mine, the subject's congenital heart condition.'

'Wait a minute, are you saying these incredible abilities have limits?'

'I'm afraid so. It's all very well releasing the superman in us but there's a good reason why he's rarely seen – the body can only withstand the stress for so long.' He put a hand on his chest. 'More research is needed but I suspect it accelerates ageing too.'

Emil now knew why, along with the rest of the orphans, Pedro would soon be dead. He steadied his resolve. 'So what happened and how did that lead to *persuading* the Arilochians to give up their children again?'

'The subject suffered a cardiac arrest and died during our struggle but not before he'd made the mistake of merging with my mind completely.' Mengele appeared to deliberately stall again. 'It meant I was able to read and influence *his* thoughts too.'

The Nazi stubbed out his cigarette. Emil gave him another straight away. 'And when I realised the devout Christian in-terpreted my probing as some kind of divine intervention, the answer to the villagers' lack of co-operation immediately became apparent.'

93

Mengele put a hand to his head. 'I made him believe I was Jesus.'

Chapter 18

'He thought you were the son of God?'

'Applying the treatment to the whole village was out of the question so I decided to subject myself to it and enter the minds of the Arilochians that way. The response was instant – they thought I'd been sent from Heaven.'

Emil considered what the villagers and the Church in particular must have thought they were getting. 'The Bible's pretty specific. What happened when God's wrath *didn't* lay waste to sinners and raise the dead as a Second Coming is supposed to?'

'There's only one thing the Church wants more than biblical prophecies to come to pass and that's non-believers converted to their cause so when I convinced a few visiting communist guerrillas to lay down their arms and worship God too...'

'And the elaborate drawings detailing how to *visit* Heaven?'

Mengele seemed reluctant to answer that. 'Smoke and mirrors to assist the belief process.'

Emil put the photograph back in front of him. 'What has this got to do with Maria's brothers?'

The making of a fresh pot of coffee was encouraged. Emil knew Mengele was stalling. Wanting the last minutes of his life to last as long as possible was the only thing he couldn't be blamed for.

'Unlike the Americans, superior intelligence didn't bother the British in the slightest. In fact, replacing their entire population with intellectual as well as physically strong supermen and women appeared to be the desired outcome.'

Emil paused refilling the percolator. 'You Nazis wanted to wipe out the Jews and we're in the middle of eradicating communists, but why on earth would a country want *all* of its citizens dead?'

'I've already told you. The British Empire is dying and they wanted to put the patient out of its misery.'

Emil thought he was being made the butt of some joke. 'Nonsense! You said yourself that the British would come to the aid of the Malvinas islanders if they had to. That doesn't sound like a nation intent on wiping itself out.'

'I also said that if you did invade the Falkland Islands, they would try to persuade you to leave and that's exactly how they intend ending the humiliation and shame of losing the world's greatest ever empire – by *persuading* the current population to commit suicide so it can be replaced.'

Emil burst out laughing. 'Well, I hope they got their money back, because you quite clearly failed!'

Mengele remained stoic. 'Dropping a hydrogen bomb might produce a similar effect but it would also lay waste to everything and make the land impossible to inhabit for hundreds of years. Far better to convince everyone to take their own lives instead.'

'Well, you did a pretty good job of convincing me to try and strangle myself earlier but by your own admission, the stress causes both parties to expire well before their time so unless...' He thought again of the doctor's graphical representation of Jacob's Ladder and how it implied a subsequent return from an ascent of it. 'The dead *can* actually be raised?'

Mengele didn't answer.

Emil shook his head. 'I'm beginning to think the British, Americans and you are all as mad and as bad as each other.' Emil dismissed it all as nonsense and got back to the purpose of his mission. 'Why did you kill six of the boys?'

Mengele became nervous again. 'Because only one was needed.'

'*One* child? All that for one single superman? Why even bother?'

'God apparently thought just the one son necessary. Perhaps the British wanted their own saviour?'

Emil dismissed that blasphemy too and picked up the portrait. 'Which one?'

The boy was pointed out. 'Juan.'

At least Emil had a name to give Maria and her mother. Now to find out if he was still alive.

'Where is he?'

'Somewhere in the UK, I suppose.'

And that statement made Emil realise he now had everything he came for. Just one job left to do. He wondered how best to ensure Mengele stayed put while the gun was retrieved. Emil was still curious about one thing, however. 'How on earth did you get the children to sit in that god-awful chair?'

Mengele may have been in fear of his life but he was still unrepentant. 'I can understand why what I've done will seem abhorrent to many but despite what's been said, I have never sought satisfaction from the suffering of others. I would have thought the orphans referring to me as 'Uncle' Joe would be enough to convince you I didn't just have the villagers' respect, I had their love too.'

Emil shifted at the uncomfortable sense of that.

'That sentiment wasn't just down to fresh grain and livestock – a steady supply of money meant the latest medical equipment and techniques. Anaesthesia and even pre-meds were always calculated to reduce anxiety to an absolute minimum.'

Emil gestured towards Mengele's scars. 'What about you? How did you manage to sedate yourself and perform surgery at the same time?'

'I didn't.'

'Then who carried out the operation?'

'My assistant.'

'Assistant? What assistant?'

The old Nazi picked up the portrait – his eyes welled.

'I think there's something Maria has yet to tell you.'

Chapter 19

Maria waved at Emil but he didn't respond. She ran towards him. He would have done the same and especially after not having seen her for weeks but not now.

She caught up, threw her arms around his neck and kissed him. The affection wasn't returned. She incorrectly guessed the reason why.

'Oh come on darling – cheer up. We both know why I have to go to the US but I'll be home twice a year and promise to write every week.' Maria gave Emil one of her faux 'damsel in distress' looks which usually got him smiling but not this time. Fake helplessness became a real concern.

'Darling – what's the matter?' She took his hand but it was pulled away.

'I found him.'

The concern appeared to intensify. 'Did you kill him?'

'No.'

The way Maria closed her eyes and drew a cross over her heart all but confirmed what Emil had always suspected but hoped could never be true. He coldly explained why he felt unable to keep his promise to Maria and her mother.

'I couldn't.' He swallowed the sense of betrayal. 'Because that would mean having to kill the equally guilty person that willingly assisted him.'

Maria stood back. 'What did he tell you?'

'Nothing. He said I should ask *you*.' Emil pushed his feelings for Maria to one side and became more policeman than future husband. 'Why do you think he would say that?'

There was a low wall a few feet from where they were standing and Maria dropped her head before shuffling towards it. Emil stayed where he was, determined not to react naturally to whatever she did or said next. Maria sat down but Emil stood his ground even though it pained him to do so.

She spoke. 'When you're young – and I mean really young – the world can seem a very frightening place.' She clutched at her bag as a distressed child would a soft toy. 'You wake up every morning wishing the horror that visited you the night before was actually a bad dream that won't ever happen again but it does – every night.'

Emil changed his mind and sat down next to her.

'To begin with you hope your distress and pleading will stop the pain but when it doesn't, there's only one thing a child raised to believe they are sinful can do and that's beg God for his forgiveness.' Maria looked at Emil. 'Isn't that what the Church teaches? Pray to God and you will be forgiven?'

She turned away again. 'But he didn't, which to me meant my sin must have been so bad, only by suffering could I be redeemed from it.'

Maria reached into her purse and took out a handkerchief to dab her eyes. 'So, like the good little girl I was so desperate to become I stopped crying, stopped pleading and just stared up at the ceiling while waiting for God to decide when I'd been punished enough.'

She withdrew an old passport from her purse and opened it.

'And then one day, *he* arrived.'

Maria placed her hand on the photograph in the same way Emil had seen Mengele place his on hers.

'My first memories were of a handsome man with a seemingly bottomless pocket of candy but it was when rumours began of Uncle Joe being the village's saviour that his appearance from nowhere started to make sense. Not just because of the miracles he performed but how he always had time for the children.' She stared ahead. 'Just like Jesus.'

The less anxious memory appeared to calm her. 'I suppose children can easily be bought with candy but it was something far more precious that made me love him just as if he were the son of God – kindness.'

She turned to Emil again. 'Can you imagine how desperate I was for a *real* father? One who didn't hurt me or abuse my mother and brothers too?'

Emil couldn't possibly empathise with what she must have suffered but nodded anyway.

Maria chuckled through her tears. 'I must have been a real pain to Uncle Joe in those early days.' She stopped laughing. 'Any excuse to get away from my rapist.'

She wiped a tear from the photograph. 'But being near Uncle Joe made me happy, so I stopped asking God for his forgiveness and began living two lives – the good of the doctor during the day and the evil of my father by night.'

She appeared to ponder what might have been. 'And if the inevitable hadn't have happened, maybe that would still be the arrangement today.'

There was no shame in what Maria said next but she hung her head all the same. 'Just after my twelfth birthday, I fell pregnant.'

Chapter 20

The revelation sickened Emil. He couldn't reconcile the horrors she must have suffered at the hands of her father with the horrors *her* hands must have perpetrated on others. He never thought it would be possible to both love and yet be repulsed by someone at the same time.

'My father flew into another one of his rages when he found out but to him, the solution was simple – my baby would become just another one of the many aborted foetuses Uncle Joe needed for his work.'

Maria lifted her head and looked into the distance. 'But he didn't understand the bond Uncle Joe and I had formed and what that would lead to.'

Her demeanour picked up for a moment. 'I'll never forget the way Uncle Joe held my hand as he not only put my mind at rest about the procedure itself but what the future held for me as his live-in housekeeper and assistant. I was so ashamed and yet at the same time so happy at the thought of actually living with the one person I knew could protect me from the evil that was my father.'

She clasped her hands together as if to plead for Emil's forgiveness. 'Can you possibly understand that?'

Emil could, but only because the alternative of perpetual

incestuous rape was too horrific to contemplate. But given the notorious Nazi doctor's history, Emil could also understand why millions of others would have serious difficulty in understanding either existence.

He swallowed before speaking. 'There's a big difference between being a housekeeper and a surgeon's assistant, Maria.'

She looked down again. 'You saw the children. They plainly needed surgery after birth but the people saw those abnormalities as God-given. Uncle Joe knew how to convince both the Church and the villagers to think differently but couldn't achieve it without my help.'

All of Emil's emotions were under pressure but it was anger that boiled over first. 'They shouldn't have been born in the first place!'

Maria coldly explained the inference of Emil's disapproval. 'Like all disabled or less worthy people, you mean?'

'No, of course not. Just those conceived *unnaturally*.'

She drew a logical conclusion from that too. 'Like my father's child perhaps?' She reminded him of their faith. 'The Catholic Church views the premature termination of *any* life to be a sin no matter what was suffered in the creation of it.'

Emil became quiet. Maria concluded with the equally logical but perhaps more disturbing revelations of what Mengele required her to do.

'Uncle Joe needed to subject himself to the operation, and I assisted him.'

Emil tried not to picture what that would have entailed but then realised he'd dreamt something similar the night before the doctor's house burnt to the ground.

The scene of his beloved ramming the head-cage device down onto Mengele filled Emil's thoughts. He knew the maniacal look on Maria's face as she repeatedly drove the drill into the Nazi's skull was just part of the nightmare, but couldn't rid himself of the vision.

It had to be confronted. 'You weren't even a teenager at the time, Maria. How could you possibly do something so horrifying?'

Maria placed a hand on his forearm. She became nervous again. 'Love, Emil. Love. When a child is suddenly released from unimaginable evil you cannot help but respond with love to what enabled that.'

She moved her hand down to his. They were both trembling. 'They say one will do anything for love and it's true.'

Emil looked deep into Maria's eyes. As a homicide officer, he had always scoffed at murderers who had suggested a similar emotion lay behind their actions but he was beginning to understand how some of them could have genuinely killed for it – killed for love.

He was wondering whether his feelings for Maria could cause him to do the same when it struck him. Why else take an unregistered gun to the so-called *evil* doctor's lair?

Emil put his arm around Maria and took the passport from her.

'He cried like a baby when I showed him your picture, you know.'

Maria responded in kind and Emil pulled her closer. He bowed to both the disturbing revelations of her childhood and the love for her he had no problem understanding.

'I guess the world is not as black and white as I like to think it is.'

Maria tilted her head up and they kissed.

Chapter 21

'You have to find him.'

'What?'

'You have to find Juan.'

'Maria, it's all but impossible to find someone missing in Argentina let alone another country.' Emil thought of the worst case. 'It's been thirteen years. He might not even be in the UK anymore – talk about looking for a needle in a haystack.'

The apparent fruitlessness didn't deter Maria. She looked up from her family's portrait. 'Then the police in England have to be contacted as soon as possible.'

Emil laughed. 'Contact the British police? Don't you read the newspapers? Their refusal to hand back the Malvinas means the junta has all but ended diplomatic relations so you can forget about any police co-operation. It has to be something pretty serious to justify contacting Interpol and I'm sorry, Maria, but the station captain would have to sanction it and I doubt Inspector Gomez would even let it get that far.'

Emil expected his fiancé to look crestfallen and an opposite reaction surprised him. 'When will you be a Captain?'

Emil became crestfallen instead. 'Maria, even if I had the necessary background, education, and political connections, it would still take at least twenty years. And that's assuming I get to the rank of Inspector first.' He put his arm around her. 'We are what we are and the situation is what it is and nothing can change that. All I know is that despite everything we've been through, we still have each other and that's the most important thing.'

Maria shrugged off the affection and stood up to face him. 'If you can't find Juan then I'm going to have to.'

Emil was about to chuckle at the ridiculous suggestion when the detective in him sensed something beyond a sisterly concern for her pseudo-sibling.

He gestured towards the portrait. 'Maria, one of the reasons why I love you so much is because, despite everything you've been through, you still care about people.'

He steeled himself for an emotionally-charged retort. 'But Juan isn't your *real* brother – he's the unnatural result of a sick experiment.'

Maria's response surprised Emil yet again. 'Tell me what Uncle Joe talked about.'

Something told Emil his love was seeking more than just a family reunion.

A disturbing thought came to him. 'Did *you* perform the brain operations on Juan and the boys?'

'No, I thought their health would ensure an escape from all that but the moment I saw their bones I knew then what I feared most had actually happened.'

She repeated the question. 'What did the doctor and you discuss *exactly*?'

Emil sighed. 'I went there to kill him, Maria. Not to have a chat.'

She sat down next to him. 'But you didn't and despite what you say, your change of heart has nothing to do with me being his assistant. What did he tell you about his work?'

'Nothing that's not either well documented or you and I haven't seen with our own eyes.' Emil slowly shook his head. 'Pure horror.'

'I'm not talking about Auschwitz or Ariloch. You didn't kill him because he made you question your own ethics.'

Given the seedier side to Emil's job as a policeman, Maria was encroaching on territory he would rather she didn't and it made him feel uncomfortable. 'I'll admit I'm no angel, Maria but if you insist on comparing my failings with those of an evil Nazi, then we need to have a serious talk.'

'He didn't just talk about *your* limitations, Emil – he made you see the failings in all of us.'

Emil was about to scoff when he picked up on the connection being made. 'According to Mengele, both the Americans and the British employed him to assist their own eugenics programmes but for different reasons.'

Maria concurred. 'Like the Nazis, the Americans want to build a master race but the British want the exact opposite – a nation of *slaves*.'

Emil regarded her as if she were as mad as the doctor. 'Why would anyone use something capable of making them invincible create a nation of unthinking sheep instead?'

'Because sheep are easier to control especially when it comes to slaughtering them. They'll happily get in line at the abattoir.'

Maria made the method of population control sound like a more efficient but just as disturbing version of Hitler's 'Final Solution'.

Emil couldn't take it in. 'Mengele likened the British Empire to a plant that had gone to seed and was now dying.' He turned to her again. 'Are you saying Juan was made to end his own life?

It doesn't make any sense.'

'He wasn't bred to be a sheep.' Maria turned to face Emil and tried to make what she had to say sound plausible. 'He's the shepherd.'

Also by Alec Birri

So, Juan Fierro must be found, but what about the fate of his twisted creator, Josef Mengele? The hunt for old Nazis escaping justice continues in...

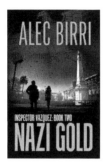

Nazi Gold: Inspector Vazquez book two

1982, and with the loss of the Falklands war causing the Argentinian junta to act like a wounded animal ready to strike, Detective Inspector Emil Vazquez is sent on an unexpected mission: assist the Brazilians in the hunt for Josef Mengele.

A surprise considering Emil knows Auschwitz's infamous Angel of Death is being protected at the highest levels. What is the junta up to now? And who is the well-dressed stranger with an even stranger accent working with the Rio de Janeiro police? CIA? MI5? Mossad?

The inspector's own police force is also acting suspiciously – Captain Gomez's niece is Emil's new deputy. Has Laura been sent to spy on him? And what's with her uncanny ability to second-guess Emil's every move? Laura seems committed enough to putting Mengele behind bars, but with key figures like the chief of police suspected Nazi sympathisers, is Emil dragging Laura into the same junta trap?

www.alecbirri.com

Printed in Great Britain
by Amazon